'I told you—'

'That you're in love with—what's his name?'

'Never you mind,' Millie said inanely.

'But I do mind. Do you have this effect on him?'

'That's chemistry,' she said desperately.

'Is it?' Adam said. 'All I know is that when I kissed you last night it was as though I'd been wanting you all my life . . .'

D0800060

Dear Reader

Summer is here at last...! And what better way to enjoy these long, long days and warm romantic evenings than in the company of a gorgeous Mills & Boon hero? Even if you can't jet away to an unknown destination with the man of your dreams, our authors can take you there through the power of their storytelling. So pour yourself a long, cool drink, relax, and let your imagination take flight...

The Editor

Jane Donnelly began earning her living as a writer as a teenage reporter. When she married the editor of the newspaper she freelanced for women's mags for a while, and wrote her first Mills & Boon romance as a hard-up single parent. Now she lives in a roses-round-the-door cottage near Stratford upon Avon, with her daughter, four dogs and assorted rescued animals. Besides writing she enjoys travelling, swimming, walking and the company of friends.

Recent titles by the same author:

SHADOW OF A TIGER

COVER STORY

BY
JANE DONNELLY

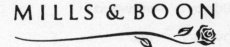

MILLS & BOON LIMITED
ETON HOUSE, 18-24 PARADISE ROAD
RICHMOND, SURREY TW9 1SR

DID YOU PURCHASE THIS BOOK WITHOUT A COVER?

If you did, you should be aware it is **stolen property** as it was reported *unsold and destroyed* by a retailer. Neither the Author nor the publisher has received any payment for this book.

All the characters in this book have no existence outside the imagination of the Author, and have no relation whatsoever to anyone bearing the same name or names. They are not even distantly inspired by any individual known or unknown to the Author, and all the incidents are pure invention.

All Rights Reserved. The text of this publication or any part thereof may not be reproduced or transmitted in any form or by any means, electronic or mechanical, including photocopying, recording, storage in an information retrieval system, or otherwise, without the written permission of the publisher.

This book is sold subject to the condition that it shall not, by way of trade or otherwise, be lent, resold, hired out or otherwise circulated without the prior consent of the publisher in any form of binding or cover other than that in which it is published and without a similar condition including this condition being imposed on the subsequent purchaser.

*MILLS & BOON and the Rose Device
are trademarks of the publisher.*

*First published in Great Britain 1994
by Mills & Boon Limited*

© Jane Donnelly 1994

*Australian copyright 1994   Philippine copyright 1994
This edition 1994*

ISBN 0 263 78581 5

*Set in Times Roman 11 on 12 pt.
01-9408-49120 C*

Made and printed in Great Britain

CHAPTER ONE

I WOULD have known you anywhere, thought Melissa Hands, looking at the man she had never seen before. He glanced across as she sidled into the room, then he went on talking to his small and attentive audience.

Millie had been about ten minutes late for work this morning. As usual she had taken her dog for an early run along the riverbank to race off his surplus energy. He had rolled in something so pungent that it had to be a fox trail and her mother would have had a nervous breakdown if Millie had left him at home all day, unwashed and reeking to high heaven.

A few minutes here or there had never mattered before but this morning the girl in Reception said, 'You'd better get up there; the new chief's arrived.'

'He isn't asking for me, is he?'

Millie had managed a grin because Adam Schofield would never have heard of Melissa Hands, and Sally had said, 'Daddy Routledge is introducing him to Editorial in the reporters' room. Everybody's supposed to be there.' She looked starstruck. 'He is a *stunner.*' Millie grimaced as she turned away.

They wouldn't miss Millie. She could wait until that gathering was over, and heaven knew she was in no hurry to get face to face with Adam Schofield. She climbed the stairs slowly and through the glass

panel from the corridor she peered in on her colleagues—reporters, sub-editors, photographers—
and the editor and the man who used to own the
Sentinel standing beside a man who dwarfed them.
Although the editor was tallish.

Nobody noticed Millie. They were all listening to
Schofield, and she supposed she wanted to hear
what he had to say. Or she could have felt that
skulking out here was cowardly; no way was she
scared of him. So she opened the door quietly and
slipped in at the back of the room.

His voice was deep and carrying, sounding reassuring. A pleasant enough voice, she supposed,
and physically there was nothing wrong with him.
As a male specimen he *was* stunning. Well over six
feet, broad-shouldered under the well cut jacket,
with high cheekbones that gave a tough, aggressive
cast to his face. But the heavy-lidded eyes gave away
nothing, and the long mouth quirked in a slight
smile.

They all seemed to be smiling with him. Probably
being reassured that nothing too drastic would
follow the takeover, although she could have told
them, Don't be taken in by what he's telling you
because he has no scruples at all.

She perched on the edge of a desk and sat with
arms folded, watching him, listening.

The sell-out had been expected but sudden. The
Sentinel was a small family-owned newspaper,
although the last owner was the last of the line, and
no sooner was it rumoured that old Daniel
Routledge was thinking of selling than contracts
were being exchanged and the *Sentinel*, its premises,

equipment and staff all came under the control of Schofield Enterprises.

Millie had missed Routledge's speech but she was sure he had rabbited on about his great-great-grandfather the founder, and the paper's standing in the neighbourhood as the voice of the local community. Because Schofield was saying that he was all for carrying on a good tradition and he was sure they knew their jobs and their readers much better than he did.

Then they were introduced to him by name and he walked round, shaking hands, recognising some of them or pretending to. Millie gripped her hands together so that she didn't have to touch him and she didn't even try to smile. A curt little nod was all she could manage but it didn't matter because the rest were falling over themselves to talk to him, and when he asked, 'Are there any questions?' they had them ready.

He assured them that their jobs were safe, no reorganisation was planned. He fielded everything lobbed at him, and although they should realise he had fooled tougher audiences than this Millie felt sorry for them. They wanted to like him. It was too damned easy for him.

But they didn't know what she knew. She had a couple of questions he wouldn't be so happy to hear. Like, Just what did you do with Sharon Ward, and how did you shut her up?

She couldn't ask that. Nor could she say, Jack Perry said to say hello. Of course you remember Jack. He's very dear to me and you nearly wiped him out.

At the door Schofield turned and she repeated
the name silently, Jack Perry, and he frowned
almost as if he heard her, although what was
probably puzzling him was that she was the only
one in the room glaring.

'Seems a reasonable bloke,' said Al, the art
editor. Alfred Chapman had worked there for the
last thirty years. Bearded and balding, his worry in
life was rheumatism. Living on a narrowboat didn't
help, and he was always talking about finding
warmer digs, just as he talked about moving somewhere where the sun was shining. He had been at
art college with Millie's father and he was one of
her favourite people. 'So why have you got a face
like thunder?' Al wanted to know.

Millie did an elaborate shrug and Lyn, the features editor, drooled, 'I could really take to him.'

'You take him,' said Millie. 'He's not my type.'
She knew they were all hoping that it wouldn't be
a bad thing to have a winner on their side. But she
couldn't say a word to explain how she knew that
Adam Schofield was never on anyone's side but his
own.

This morning he was walking around the building
with Daddy Routledge and John Adams, the editor,
and it was pure chance that Millie kept meeting him.
The premises weren't big and she had to go up to
Photography and down into the library and there
he was in both. No sooner did she walk in than she
walked out again. And in the corridor he seemed
to be coming round every blessed corner she turned.

This morning the three-storey building that
housed the *Sentinel* newspaper was riddled with
Adam Schofield, and she was glad when she could

get away with her assignments for the day tucked into her shoulder-bag.

She stood in the doorway, looking out into the pale sunshine that was trying to break through the clouds, and would not have been surprised if his shadow had fallen over her. This had to be a brief visit. He wouldn't be here tomorrow. 'Come on,' she said to the photographer who was off to the animal rescue centre with her, 'let's get the pictures of the barn owl.'

She walked home from the office that night. With it being a market town, parking was never easy, and she enjoyed walking. Along the river was the prettier, longer way, through the streets only took twenty minutes or so, and she stopped at the first phone box but the number she dialled was engaged.

Millie's home was a pretty Edwardian building, detached, with a small front garden and lawn at the back leading down to the river. She had always lived here and nothing much had changed in her memory. The furniture was good, elegant, the rooms were spacious. It was a delightful house and a perfect setting for her mother, who called from the drawing-room as Millie opened the front door, 'Is that you, dear?'

'Yes,' called back Millie, fending off the joyous onslaught of the huge black dog.

'We're in here.'

The open doorway framed Elena Hands like a picture, as she sat feet up on the *chaise-longue*, tea on the little table, and her visitor in a brocade-covered armchair putting on a brave smile.

Millie knew what was ailing Barbara. Most of her circle knew that her husband was having an affair with his secretary, who was twenty years younger, and Elena was dispensing tea and sympathy with the sweet understanding of a woman who knew that nothing like that could ever happen to her.

It made Millie angry. If her advice had been asked she would have said, 'You're well rid,' but nobody asked her and Barbara Mottram was always telling herself that one day he would change his ways.

But her husband was a womaniser who would cheat as long as he had the strength and the money, and Millie couldn't sit quietly listening to this without feeling a hypocrite herself. She said, 'Hello, Barbara, how nice to see you,' and went upstairs, unhitching the phone and taking it with her.

The biggest room upstairs was her father's studio. Light streamed into that from the northern windows and her mother usually kept the door open. Millie closed it now and closed her own bedroom door behind her, sat on the bed and dialled again.

This time a man said, 'Perry Promotions.'

'Hi,' said Millie, 'it's me. He's arrived.' There was a short silence and she asked, 'Can you talk?'

'Yes. How did he strike you?'

'Just as you said, he's got them all eating out of his hand.' She added cynically, 'Well, he would have, wouldn't he? He's the boss.'

'But not you?'

'What do you think?'

'That's my girl.'

'I didn't enjoy having him around.' That was an understatement. Being under the same roof as the man had kept her nerves jangling. 'He shouldn't be here too long but there'll probably be changes and I don't think I'm going to enjoy them either.'

Jack's chuckle was wry. 'If you get the chance, poison his coffee.' And she forced a giggle.

'I don't think I'll be making coffee or anything else for him.'

'Look out for yourself. Look after yourself.'

'You too.' She always had this warm feeling of togetherness when she was phoning Jack, as though he was in the room with her.

'Keep in touch,' he said, and she could hear him smiling because this was one of their joke sayings. So was her reply.

'Bank on it.' She switched the phone off and took it back to its cradle in the hall.

She couldn't settle to anything. She hadn't realised how much meeting the man had disturbed her, and she didn't disturb easily. In the kitchen she gave the dog most of the meal that had been left for her to heat up in the microwave, and then went along to the drawing-room where her mother and her mother's friend were still talking and clinking teacups.

'I'm taking the dog out,' she told them.

'Try to keep him out of the river this time.' Elena gave a fastidious shudder. 'He came back soaking wet this morning, shaking himself all over.'

'Water could have been the least of your worries,' said Millie. 'He came back smelling like a cesspool; you got him after I'd fumigated him,' and Elena and Barbara screeched together.

This had been a wet month. No Indian summer this year. It was not raining now but off the path the riverbanks were muddy, and keeping the dog away from the river was a problem. The Labrador in him gave him an affinity with water, he loved it, and Millie hurled a ball, which he retrieved tirelessly, across the rough grasses of the meadows.

She loved the river too. She had a little cabin cruiser moored along here that she had bought with a small legacy from a great-aunt. It was a canal or riverboat but sometimes she would lie on the bunk, watching the stars through the porthole, pretending she was all alone on some faraway deep dark ocean.

Just beyond her cruiser the river widened around an islet, and that was where Al's narrowboat had a permanent mooring. He might not be there. A wisp of smoke rose from the thin tin chimney. He always kept the stove going and most evenings he spent in his local pub, but Millie was in no hurry to get back home and listen to Barbara making allowances for her cheating husband.

She had been strolling over the narrow bridge to the tiny island for years. A previous boat had sunk and Alf had replaced it, but that was before the damp had settled in his bones and river life had lost its appeal. Millie would like to buy it from him and live here like a water gypsy, but she hadn't the money and her mother needed her around the house.

The dog got over the bridge first and plunged into the rushes following the trail of a rat or a vole. In grabbing him by the collar and hauling him back Millie stepped into the mud herself, water squelching over her shoes up to her ankles.

Feet like these, cold and sticky and heavy, would take the pleasure out of walking, and if Al was not at home she hoped he had done what he usually did, not bothered to lock up, so that she could dry off by his stove. She stepped on to the deck and down the steep steps to the unlocked door of the galley. Sitting on the steps, she took off her shoes, said 'Stay' very firmly to the dog, and padded through into the long, narrow saloon.

At the far end a big Welsh dresser was the divider, with a bedroom and a bathroom beyond; and the fire burned brightly behind the perspex doors of the stove.

'Are you here, Al?' she called. The warm glow was lovely. She went down in front of the stove, warming her face and her hands then taking off her coat and beginning to peel off her tights.

'Good evening,' said Adam Schofield, and she nearly lost her balance, lurching on one leg and croaking,

'Where's Al?'

'He'll be along soon.'

She was breathless, and not just from the heat of the stove nor because she looked ridiculous hopping around on dirty feet, but because everything seemed to be closing in on her. The narrowboat was only seven feet wide but she had never felt claustrophobic in it before. Now with Adam Schofield standing there it was as though she was trapped.

'I came to dry off at Al's stove,' she babbled. 'We've been in the river.'

'We?'

'Me and my dog.' She backed to the galley door to let the dog in. Not that she needed protection. Support perhaps. He was a large animal and until she stopped feeling dizzy she could hang on to him. Finding Adam Schofield here had really shaken her.

'Late in the day for paddling, isn't it?' he said.

'Not for this one; he thinks he's a water buffalo.'

The dog was a hotchpot of a mongrel, with Alsatian and Labrador easiest to spot. Built like a timber wolf, he could be frightening, but he was a dog who loved life and almost everybody. He came in jauntily, swishing a long plumed tail, and flopped down in front of the stove.

Schofield laughed. 'And what was your excuse for ending in the river?'

'I'm an idiot,' she admitted. 'He'd have got out, he always does, but I grabbed him and stepped into the mud. Where *is* Al?'

'Gone to make a phone call.' The nearest phone was in the pub but why had Al left Adam Schofield here? She looked surprised and he answered her unspoken question. 'I'm getting the feel of the place.'

'Why?'

'I'm thinking of taking a lease on it.'

'Why?'

'I may be staying round here for a while.'

That knocked her back again. She knew that his company had bought other local property but she hadn't expected him to settle in the area, and if he had done, surely a top hotel or apartment were more in his line? This was cluttered and scruffy and the amenities were spartan. Adam Schofield, immaculately groomed and expensively tailored, looked wildly out of place to Millie.

'And I like narrowboats.'

She almost gasped, 'But you can't stay here,' then gulped most of that back and stammered, 'But— we'll be neighbours.' He waited until she went on, 'My boat's moored opposite,' and then he smiled and no one had ever said that he was short on charm.

'A very good reason for taking it,' he said, and she thought incredulously, He likes me.

Most folk did. She was young, attractive, likeable. Men often made passes, and what he had just said was the sort of thing anyone might say. But there was more to it. A sudden heightened awareness between them that made sense with her because it was antagonism, but in him it was interest. He was intrigued by her, and the last thing she wanted was Adam Schofield wondering what went on in her mind or lusting after her body.

She had to get away from eyes that had become probing and from the stillness in him as he stood there, watching her. Perhaps he sensed that she was his enemy. He was searching for something and she had to break away before he found it. She said, 'I'll get a towel.'

The dog raised its head as she went towards the opening by the Welsh dresser and Schofield asked, 'What's his name?'

'Flower.'

'You are joking.' Nobody believed it, and when she called him to heel in public places she had them falling about laughing because anything less flowerlike was hard to imagine.

'He was a very pretty puppy,' she said. At a few weeks old he had had a face like a velvety flower, but he had rapidly grown out of that.

'Weren't we all?' said Schofield.

She went through the bunkroom into the bathroom and grabbed a towel. Water had to be carried here from the tap on the riverbank, another thing that was getting too much for Al, so she would rub her feet as clean as possible and take the towel home for laundering.

She leaned against the side and rubbed away, and wondered what Adam Schofield had looked like in his younger days. She hadn't changed much. Photographs showed a bright-eyed child and she still had a happy face.

She wouldn't hang around waiting for Al. She would put on her sodden shoes again and go home, but she didn't want to give the impression that she was harassed or anxious or let him feel he was driving her away. She was a news reporter. Sometimes she had to mix with people she disliked intensely and they never suspected. She could surely do the same with him for a little while longer. She might even get him talking about the *Sentinel*. She was steadier now; her guard was up.

She went back into the saloon and said, 'You were never pretty.'

'Never,' he said.

He was sitting on the sagging sofa and she edged past to collect her muddy shoes, bringing them back and balancing them on top of the stove. That would do the leather no good but it should dry them in record time. She draped her tights over the fireguard and he said, 'I'm sure Al would be offering you a drink.'

'I don't go much for Al's hard stuff.' There was a half-empty bottle of whisky on a low chest that served as a table, and she almost joked, Don't let Al do the pouring for you—he never hears anyone say 'when'. That showed she was still jittery, nearly telling that to Al's future employer, and anyhow Adam Schofield had ice in his veins—nobody was going to crack his self-control.

'There's coffee,' he said.

'Have you tried it?'

Al brewed up and kept coffee hot in a brown glazed pot on the top of the stove. It was thick and dark and very strong, but Schofield said, 'I've had worse. There's a touch of the Turkish about it.'

She remembered Jack saying, 'Poison his coffee,' and almost giggled hysterically because this was crazy. She said, 'There's a touch of something that can take the roof off your mouth. It's taken me years to get used to it.'

'That's better.'

'What is?'

'You've been so tight-lipped up to now I was beginning to wonder if you had teeth.'

She bared them, white and even, in a fixed grin, 'Oh I have teeth all right, but I thought there was enough smiling being done this morning. Somehow I don't see you as a philanthropist come to keep us all happy on the *Sentinel*.'

'Are you all happy?'

She unhooked a mug from the dresser and poured herself coffee. 'We get along,' she said. 'They're a good bunch.'

'How long have you worked there?'

'Four years.'

'How long have you lived here?'

'All my life.' She wasn't sitting down on the sofa beside him. She took a wooden armchair that was rickety unless you knew how to balance on it.

'Not on the boat?'

'No, I live near the river going out of town, in a solid old-fashioned house.' She nursed the hot mug in both hands and felt the warmth of the stove on her bare legs. She had good legs, long and slim, but she crossed her ankles and tucked her feet under the chair. She was uncomfortable, sprawling in front of Adam Schofield.

'You could be a mine of local information.' His voice was drawling and lazy, as if he couldn't be more relaxed.

'I surely am.' But she wouldn't be passing any information on to him, and she asked, her voice lazy as his, 'What are your plans for our paper?'

'Have you any suggestions?'

'We give the public what they seem to want. Weddings and funerals, sales of work, magistrates' courts, council meetings. Pictures of themselves and their friends.'

'Don't you get bored with that?'

One day she might move on somewhere more exciting, but for the present she was content. She drank another gulp of her coffee and looked at him from under long dark lashes. 'What I write in my spare time isn't boring at all,' she said. 'It's very steamy, sexy stuff.'

'A novel?'

'Aha.' She smiled, lips together, tight-lipped as if she was holding in a secret. 'Well,' she said, 'it makes a change from boring old routine.'

Now he was going to ask her about her book, and she would have to say she didn't discuss the plot, or invent one. It was playing with fire and she must stop making private and bitter jokes that he couldn't possibly understand.

'Where do you usually live?' she asked, although she knew already. He would have been astounded to learn how much she did know about him and his goings-on. Or that while she sat here, chatting and joking like any bright and friendly girl with an intelligent, attractive man, she could have spat in his face.

Flower heard Al first. The dog raised his head, ears pricked, then got up, tail wagging, and was at the door into the galley before they heard the footsteps on the deck and creaking down the steps.

Al beamed at them both, and it was a cosy scene in the fireglow from the stove. 'I'm drying my feet,' said Millie.

Schofield stood up. 'You didn't tell me Millie was a neighbour.'

'I was coming to that,' said Al. 'That was going to be the clincher.' He lit one of the oil lamps, turning up the wick and applying a match. 'You know how these things work?' Schofield nodded. 'I can move out any time,' said Al. Millie knew he had been offered digs in a centrally heated bungalow; he must have been phoning there.

'I must be moving myself,' she said. She took her tights from behind the Welsh dresser and came back to put on her still mud-encrusted shoes and her coat. 'I shall miss you being here,' she said to Al. 'There never was a time when you weren't here.'

She wouldn't be crossing the little bridge to visit Adam Schofield and Al said gruffly, 'I'll miss you too, Millie.' He told Schofield, 'Her father used to bring her over here before she could walk. We were students together, her father and me, and that's going back a lifetime. Now he *was* a painter. I've always been a bloody good craftsman but he was an artist. You must get her to show you some of his work.'

'I'd like that,' said Schofield, who could hardly have said anything else, and Millie smiled and thought, What for? I don't want to hear his opinion.

'I'll walk back with you,' he said, and she said hastily,

'No need—Flower's a good guard dog and we're a law-abiding lot round here.'

'I probably go your way. I'm staying at Alderson Towers.' That was a hotel out of town. Walking towards it, along the river, he would pass Millie's house, and all she could say was,

'All right, then.'

Over the bridge she pointed out her boat and asked, 'How long will you be staying?'

'I'm renting it for six months.'

'You're going to live on it?'

'Not all the time.'

The small talk in her was drying up. The narrowboat was warm and full of friendly vibes, it had been easier to play-act in there, but out here night was falling and the familiar river paths seemed like a strange country. The tall man striding along beside her was a sinister stranger when all she knew of him was dark and shadowed.

They walked without talking, but if he thought this was a comfortable silence he couldn't have been farther from the truth. On her part she was quiet because her throat had closed up and her stomach was knotted with tension, and she let Flower run ahead so that she could hurry herself.

At the gate to her garden she said, 'Here we are,' and was surprised that came out easily; she had expected to croak. 'Will you come in for another coffee?' she said, which surprised her even more because she hadn't meant to say that.

'I'd like to, but I'm expecting a phone call.'

She was glad he was. As she opened the gate he asked, 'Will you have dinner with me?'

'What?' She'd heard. That was a gasp.

'Dinner, tomorrow night?'

'All right.' She couldn't say, I'd rather starve, after she had been chatting away to him in the boat.

'Seven o'clock? I'll call for you.'

'I'll come to the hotel.' She didn't want him in the house. Her mother would meet him and be impressed and want to talk about him and that was a complication Millie could do without.

He said, 'I'll look forward to it. Goodnight.'

'That will be—nice. Goodnight.' She got through the gate and walked across the lawn wondering what the hell she was doing.

She didn't want to get involved with Adam Schofield but here she was agreeing to present herself at his hotel and spend the evening with him, eating and drinking at his expense and presumably singing for her supper. On a list of men she would hate to date he would be near the top, and yet she had just said, 'That would be nice.' She had to be

drunk on caffeine or brain-washed or going gaga
at twenty-three.

There was no one downstairs and she found her
mother upstairs in the studio. 'I thought I'd have
an early night,' Elena said. She tired easily; she had
always been delicate. 'I'm just saying goodnight to
your father.'

It was years since Colin Hands had put aside his
brushes, got into his car and crashed on the
motorway. Paint had hardened, brushes had dried,
but nothing had been moved in here since the day
he died. Elena still kept the memory of him so alive
that he might have been in the next room. Now she
said, 'Talking to somebody like Barbara makes me
realise how lucky I was.'

'We were,' said Millie. 'What shall I bring you
up?'

'Just a hot milk.'

'Right. Twenty minutes?'

She went downstairs again, taking the phone into
the kitchen with her, closing the kitchen door and
tapping Jack's number. He answered almost at once
and she said, 'The craziest thing has just happened;
he's asked me for a date.'

'Who has?' He knew who was talking, he had
to realise who she was talking about but, like her,
he was finding it hard to believe.

'Adam Schofield. To have dinner with him
tomorrow.'

'On your own?'

'Yes. I've just met him again and he fancies me.'

'He probably does. So do most of them, don't
they?'

'Often enough, but him, for Pete's sake!'

Jack laughed softly. 'Now that opens up some possibilities. What did you say?'

'I said yes.' She pulled a bewildered face. 'And I'm still wondering why. I suppose I thought I might learn what's happening to the *Sentinel*.' Although when she'd said yes she hadn't stopped to think at all. 'He might talk to me,' she added.

'Anything he had to say in confidence would be fascinating stuff, but watch how *you* talk to *him*,' Jack warned her. 'He's got a mind like a steel trap. One wrong word, one look, could give the game away.'

Schofield had suggested she might be bored. Perhaps she was, and this was a dangerous game to be playing, but suddenly she was smiling. 'Oh I'll be careful. You know how well I can keep a secret.'

'Oh, I do.' He laughed again, louder, jubilantly. 'This could be our lucky break. Between us we could have him . . .'

CHAPTER TWO

AFTER she had taken the hot milk in to her mother, Millie stood for a moment in the open doorway of her father's studio. There were unfinished paintings in there. The one he had been working on when he died was still on the easel. Ironically, it had been a self-portrait; the vague unformed features were ghost-like and soon after his death Millie, as a schoolgirl of sixteen, had put it away.

Her mother had replaced it and sobbed, 'We must not change anything in here. You must understand that.'

Millie had said that she did, because she had idolised her father too. He had been so handsome and so talented. Everyone still said how talented he was, and she hoped that Adam Schofield wouldn't follow up Al's suggestion that he should come here and look over Colin Hands' work.

She didn't want him in the studio. She wasn't in it much herself these days, although she knew that it would always be the most important room in the house for her mother.

Millie had been born in this house. Even after her father's death it was where she had felt safe and sure about most things until one day in late summer, just over two years ago, when the earth had shaken beneath her feet and nothing was ever quite the same again.

Her mother was on holiday with friends—she was always glad about that—and Amy, who came in to do most of the housework and the cooking, was out shopping.

The doorbell rang and Millie went to answer it with Flower. A young man stood there, boyish, bright-eyed, with mid-brown hair and an attractively diffident smile, enquiring, 'This is where Colin Hands, the artist, used to live?'

She said, 'Yes—what can we do for you?'

'I've just acquired a painting of his. His address was on a label at the back.'

'My father died five years ago.' He hadn't been famous. Someone picking up one of his paintings might not have known about the accident, but maybe this man did because he didn't commiserate.

He said, 'It was a good painting, a portrait. I'd like to have bought more.'

'Sorry.' She shook her head. 'We do have some pictures, but there's nothing for sale, although if you'd like to see them you're welcome.'

She was immediately at ease with him, and Flower sensed this and didn't bark. The man thanked her and stepped into the hall where there was a series of water-colour scenes on the wall. He stopped in front of each, as she explained more or less when they had been painted. Then she asked, 'Would you like to see his studio?'

'Very much.'

'It's just as it was.' She had been proud of it then. She had felt close to her father in here. 'That's a self-portrait,' she said, 'but you have to have known him to recognise it. Have you seen *Gone with the Wind*?'

'Yes.'

'Well, he looked like Leslie Howard. By the way, I'm Melissa Hands.'

'Jack Perry.' His tone was preoccupied, then he turned from the easel and looked hard at her and she stared back because something about him seemed familiar.

He seemed to hesitate, then he said, 'It's the eyes.'

'What is?' She had blue-grey eyes that were flecked with green, and his eyes were flecked too.

'I think I'm probably your brother.'

'What?' That came out like a whinny because she had no breath in her.

'He's your father, isn't he?' Without turning again, he indicated the easel by a head movement and she nodded dumbly. 'Well he seems to be mine.'

Instinctively she glanced towards the open door, although she knew that her mother was a hundred miles away. 'You'd better sit down,' he said, and he told her afterwards that she had gone white to the lips.

She felt her way to a chair blindly and sat down heavily. 'I knew he was dead,' he said. 'I wanted to see if there were any other paintings and this house seemed a good place to start.'

She cut through his words shrilly. 'What do you mean he was your father? I mean, who told you— how do you know?'

'Nobody told me. My mother died last month; I've just finished going through her papers and there were letters. How old are you?'

'Twenty-one.'

'I'm twenty-three.' Her parents had been married three years when she was born. This must have been during the first year of their married life, when they were almost on honeymoon still, and she couldn't believe it. But he went on, 'My mother married the man I always thought was my father when she was pregnant. He was older than she was and he thought I was his.'

She had to swallow twice before she could ask, 'What did—the letters say?'

'Do you want to see them?'

'*No*,' and then, because she had no choice, 'Yes.'

'I'll get them.'

She went downstairs with him and walked into the drawing-room as he went through the front door. Ben was out there mowing the lawn. He had been their twice-a-week gardener as long as she could remember, just as Amy had turned up every day. Both of them had known her parents before she was born and she wondered if they knew about this man called Jack Perry who said his father was Colin Hands.

When she sat down, Flower whined and put his chin on her knees, and she clutched the rough fur of his neck convulsively, and tried to stop shaking.

Jack Perry came back carrying a briefcase, put it on the low table in front of her, opened it and took out a newspaper cutting. She read the headline: 'Artist in Motorway Death Pyre'. There was a photograph of a burned-out car and a report of her father's death.

She put it aside, closed her eyes, and bit hard on her lip, and the man said gently, 'My mother was suddenly taken ill when that happened. For a while she seemed to be having a nervous breakdown. I keep a diary; I know the date.'

So Millie's mother had not been the only woman who mourned the death of a lover. 'Were they still seeing each other?' Millie's voice was thin and childlike.

'If they were, nobody knew about it, I'm sure of that. And that her husband thought I was his son. He died three years ago.'

He held out two letters and she accepted them wordlessly. They were both typed and dated. Both love letters, but the first was asking her to have an abortion. It could be arranged discreetly and all the expenses met. The second was saying that she must do what she thought best, she knew what she meant and would always mean to him. They were signed 'C', and she dropped them back into the open briefcase.

She nodded at the photograph of a young man who could have been a stand-in for Leslie Howard, sitting at a café table, smoking a cigarette. And a pen and ink sketch of the head and shoulders of a girl was her father's work. She said, 'Yes,' to that and after a moment, 'She was very pretty.'

He had lost her recently and she felt a wave of sympathy for him when she saw the grief in his face. He looked up at the full-length oil-painting of Elena over the mantelpiece.

'Is that your mother?'

'Yes.'

'He could pick them,' he said wryly.

This had been painted in the early days of the marriage, but Elena's fair, fragile beauty was almost unchanged today. She looked as though a good gust of wind would blow her away and soon after the accident their family doctor had warned Millie, 'It's hard, because you're only a slip of a girl yourself, but you'll have to look after her, Millie.'

She said, in horror, 'It will kill her. She worshipped him.'

'There's no need for her to know.'

This had seemed such shattering news that she had felt it would reach everyone who knew them by the end of the week. But he was saying, 'I've told nobody. I didn't mean to tell anyone I found in this house either. I've been called a bastard often enough; I don't need to prove it.'

She wondered what he meant by that, but when he indicated the suitcase and its contents and said, 'That's all the proof there is,' she begged,

'Can I get rid of it?'

'You can do what you like with it,' he said.

It was a warm summer's day, there was no fire in here but the Aga burned in the kitchen and she gathered up the pathetic little sheaf of papers, took them into the kitchen and dropped them in the stove. When small flames curled around them she had a last fleeting glimpse of the young man who had been her father, and the pretty girl who was the mother of her brother, before they blackened into ashes.

Then she breathed freely for the first time in minutes. She was so relieved that this was staying a secret that the shock was beginning to wear off, and when she went back into the drawing room she was smiling. Weakly, but it was a smile.

She tried it out, 'My brother. I can't tell anybody but I like the sound of it.'

He smiled too. 'Sister sounds all right. Are you the only one?'

'Yes.'

'Tell me about yourself. No rings. Not married?'

'Not yet. You?'

'Not yet. You work for a living?'

'Of course. He wasn't rich. There isn't any real money.'

He grinned. 'I wasn't thinking of blackmail.' And she fell over herself to stress that she knew that. She told him,

'I'm a reporter on our local newspaper. What do you do?'

He was a publicist, getting stories about his clients into newspapers, booking them on to TV shows, arranging lucrative publicity deals.

By now they were sitting facing each other and talking non-stop. His clients were a colourful bunch and most of the stories were sensational, from kiss-and-tells to wising up reporters on corruption and scandals.

She recognised some of the names he mentioned. She remembered the stories. She understood what he meant when he said he had been called a bastard, especially by those who didn't want their story told.

From their work they went on with other questions and answers, learning all they could of each other, making up for the lost years.

After a while she asked, 'Will you stay for a meal?'

Ben was still in the garden. She saw him through the window and wondered if he would see the resemblance between herself and Jack.

Jack checked his watch. 'I have to be off.' He stood up, 'But will you come and stay with me?'

She looked doubtful. 'Who would you say I was?' And he agreed.

'That is a problem.'

She bit her lip again. 'I don't want anyone starting talking. My mother's not strong. If you turned up from the first year of her marriage she couldn't take it.'

'But we will keep in touch?'

'Bank on it. I'll like having a secret brother.'

'By the way, my name's John Colin Perry. She always said she liked the name Colin.'

'You never used it?'

'No, and I'm glad now that I didn't. He was a good artist but he was a rat.'

She had always thought that her father was wonderful but she couldn't defend him this time and she said miserably, 'How could he have been such a hypocrite?'

Jack laughed harshly, 'That's no surprise; the world's crawling with cheats. I meet them every day in my business. You're a reporter and you haven't realised that? What kind of paper are you working for?'

Not his kind, that was for sure. She said, 'Oh, ours is a cosy little number. We take folk at face value.'

He produced a card from his wallet. 'Well if you come across anything that rates a wider public, let me know. Write to me anyway; I want to hear what's happening to you.'

She went to the front door with him. This time she was the one who said, 'Keep in touch' and he said, 'Bank on it,' and put an arm around her.

Impulsively she hugged him and he kissed her cheek.

She watched his car leave with mixed emotions. She was shattered by her father's betrayal, but part of her was glad that Jack had found her. She had always missed not having a brother or a sister and Jack was her brother all right. He was right about other things too. The world was crawling with cheats when her own father had been one.

She closed the studio door that night instead of leaving it ajar. This was her secret and Jack's but it changed Millie. From that day she was not as trusting as she used to be. Not quite the dewy-eyed idealist any longer, although nobody seemed to notice the difference.

Between twenty-one and twenty-three Millie enjoyed life. She liked her work, she had good friends and her love-life was generally satisfactory. Nobody gave her a hard time and most of her friends thought they knew Millie Hands really well. Because what you saw with Millie was what you got.

So it was, up to a point, but the one who knew her best was the man she had only seen four times in the last two years. Most weeks they spoke on the phone. Sometimes they wrote to each other. They were brother and sister, living and working apart but keeping in touch as though they had grown up together, and there had always been a bond of deep family affection.

Next morning Millie woke with that hollow feeling you got when you were booked in with your dentist.

You knew this was not going to be a good day and as you opened your eyes you remembered why.

When she remembered, her eyes went wide because it was incredible. She was dating Adam Schofield, and dislike was not strong enough a word for the way she felt about him. When they'd heard whose company was taking over the *Sentinel* she had felt ill. On the phone she had said to Jack, 'I'll chuck my job, I'll go freeelance; I can't work for him.' But she had decided to wait and see.

She hadn't thought he was likely to be around much and she'd thought she could keep out of his way, but yesterday she had been coming up against him wherever she went and tonight she had a date with him. This morning that seemed as foolhardy as walking into a hungry lion's cage for supper.

He wasn't going to confide in her; why should he? He'd asked her out because he fancied her and he must think she felt the same because she had said yes.

There would be table-talk over dinner, but what would happen afterwards, if he made a real pass?

She shivered under a warm shower, imagining him touching her, and downstairs she stood by the phone wondering what excuse she could give for phoning his hotel and calling off.

In the end she didn't call because of course she was panicking over nothing. On a first date it would be easy to say no. Most men would expect that these days. A second might be getting in deeper but there wouldn't be a second and this was no big deal. This was just a bad joke, and she walked into the office to find that Al, in ahead of her, had told them all that Adam Schofield had walked her home last night.

When they wanted to know what happened she said, 'Nothing—what were you expecting? He went my way because it was the way to his hotel from the river.'

She kept quiet about her date; the women would have been fascinated there. 'Lucky thing,' they would have said enviously, and it was crazy that the one female on the staff who couldn't stand the sight of Adam Schofield was the one who would be getting closest to him tonight.

But knowing what was waiting for her loomed over her all day like a stormcloud. She kept looking at her watch, getting more and more worked up as time went by.

Getting ready that evening, she took a long, leisurely bath that should have relaxed her, but the face that looked back from the mirror was white and tense. Almost *scared*, and that was stupid. She didn't want to meet him and pretend she was enjoying his company, but there was nothing to be scared about; he could do her no harm. And she took a bright orange dress out of her wardrobe and put some colour on her face, so that she looked vivid and confident even if she was shaking inside.

She took her little Fiesta. It was a short journey, but driving she could stay with one glass of wine and keep her wits about her.

The hotel had been built as the home of a Victorian industrialist, although its Gothic towers and pointed windows made it seem older and, in the gloaming and for the first time, it looked forbidding and ominous to Millie.

Until now she had rather liked the place. She had had some happy times here; an engagement party a couple of months ago had been a riotous success. But now, as she parked her Fiesta alongside a Honda Accord, she looked across at the grey towers against the darkening sky and thought, It looks like Bluebeard's castle.

She tried to smile at that but she couldn't deny the butterflies in her stomach nor the way her heart was hammering. People were everywhere, in the car park, in the huge entrance hall, but as soon as she stepped through the great doors she saw Adam Schofield and the others became shadowy.

She stood still, fighting an urge to run for it as he came towards her. 'I'm glad you could come,' he said, and she thought, Don't touch me. So long as you don't touch me I can get through this.

She smiled a brilliantly false smile. 'Lovely to see you again,' she said gaily. She could feel heads turning and eyes following them as he led her towards the lift, and she knew she wasn't the one they were watching,

You're an arrogant swine, she thought bitterly. You walk through here as if you own the place and I wouldn't be surprised if you do.

The restaurant was on the ground floor. In the lift she asked, 'Where are we going?'

'I've got a suite.'

'Of course you have. You don't own this hotel, do you?'

'No. Why?'

'I just wondered.' She kept smiling. Suffocating claustrophobia had hit her the moment she stepped in here with him, but she kept smiling. Walking along the corridor, their footsteps silent on the thick carpeting, she thought this was like some weird dream that could turn into a nightmare, her heading for a hotel room with Adam Schofield.

'What kind of a day have you had?' he asked her.

'Hilarious. One silver wedding, one jumble sale. How about you?'

'Wheeling and dealing.'

Double-dealing, she thought. Who and what have you put the screws on today? 'Very lush,' she said as he opened the door.

It was a large sitting-room, with a big stone fire-place, furnished in keeping with the four-star status of the hotel. In a round turret window was a chair and a table with papers on it. She wouldn't have minded a quick look through them.

Another table was laid for two, and two doors were closed so the bathroom and bedroom were out of sight. This was like eating in a private house. She would have been more comfortable in the crowded restaurant but she could cope with this.

She sat down and looked at the man sitting opposite, and although she felt she knew his features well this close scrutiny was like looking at him for the first time. He was dangerous, she knew that from Jack. But the eyes, the set of the mouth, seemed the hardest she had ever encountered, and her own mouth went dry.

He poured white wine and she needed a sip before she could say, 'I'm driving,' and that amused him.

'All of a five-minute run. Of course this wouldn't be an excuse?'

'It might be,' she admitted. 'I wouldn't want to get talking too much.'

'About what?'

They were making a joke of it although had he but known it it was no joke at all. She didn't laugh, wrinkling her nose. 'I might get indiscreet about— I don't know. Did you ask me here to grill me about the *Sentinel* or the narrowboat or something?'

'No,' he said. 'Be as indiscreet as you like; it will go no further than these four walls.'

'I may be a simple country girl——' she put on a wide-eyed look of idiot innocence '—but I believe that like I believe in the tooth-fairy.'

Food was brought in and served. Creamed chicken breast stuffed with crab and side dishes: minted new potatoes, mangetout peas, half a dozen different delicious looking salads.

At first she could hardly get down a mouthful although she should have been hungry, she had eaten nothing all day, she had been too worked up about tonight's ordeal. And it was still an ordeal; she was still nervous as a watchful cat.

But he was very good company. He was funny and flattering. He made her laugh and he told her she was beautiful.

He had asked about her family and she told him that her mother was a beauty. 'Of course,' he said.

'Why of course?'

'You're beautiful.'

'No, I'm not.' She wasn't being coy. Compared to Elena she was nothing special. 'But thank you,' she said. 'I'm working on it.'

She didn't look much like her mother or her father. She looked more like her brother, and that made her remember Sharon Ward.

Adam Schofield had been that girl's lover and it was like a kick in the stomach imagining the hard lean body stripped of the expensive suiting. Warmth rose under her own skin, burning on her cheekbones, and she began to tell him about the jumble sale that afternoon, and the vicar's wife's new coat being sold for two pounds fifty.

He would think the compliment had embarrassed her because she was making high drama of the jumble sale tale, and when they finished smiling over that she asked, 'When are you moving into the boat?'

'Tomorrow.'

'I wouldn't have thought it was your scene. It's rough living on a narrowboat. This seems more like you.' She surveyed the room, which stood for luxury and service.

'You think so?'

She looked down at his hands. The skin was smooth and tanned, the nails well kept, but they were strong hands. They could handle a boat. They could probably handle a runaway horse, and they could handle a woman. She wondered if he was rough as a lover and thought not. He was too clever for that, although he was brutal enough when it came to the end of the affair.

She had taken strawberries from a bowl of fruit and was eating them in her fingers, dipping them into sugar on her plate, enjoying the squashy feeling of the fruit and the sweetness of the sugar on her tongue. Her own hands were strong and she had a tender, arousing touch. She had had men moaning for more under her sensuous stroking, but she couldn't see herself even reaching out to touch Adam Schofield's face, let alone running fingertips over the hard contours of bare shoulders and down the long ridge of his spine.

The phone rang for a third time. Twice before he had murmured, 'Excuse me,' and answered, speaking briefly. She thought it had been one man, one woman, going by the slight difference in the tone of his voice, although she could have imagined that.

This time he said, 'I'll be right down,' and to her, 'There's someone waiting I must see. About five minutes. You'll be all right?'

Of course she would, sitting here eating strawberries. 'Of course,' she said.

Now's your chance, Jack would say. Take a quick shuftie at those papers and see if you can find anything dodgy.

She got up and went to the windows in the round tower. Down below lights sparkled like diamonds in the trees, and edging a bridge over a little stream was a string of green lights like an emerald necklace.

She turned her back on the windows and leaned over the desk. The top paper was about a planning application, change of use from an antiques market to a wine bar, in another town, and she picked up that paper to flick through the rest.

That was when she realised how sugar sticky her fingers were and hurried back to the table to rub most of it off on a napkin. A little sugar edged one of the papers, she coaxed that away, and then she

choked because on the top page was a strawberry
juice thumbprint, vivid as blood.

She might as well have signed her name. If she
had been sure there was time she could have tried
washing it off in the bathroom, but that might make
a worse mess and if she was caught she would look
guilty and underhand as hell. The only thing for it
was confession.

She stood at the window until he came back—
he was quick, she wouldn't have managed to do
more than start swilling it under the tap—and she
said, 'I've put a strawberry smudge on your papers.
I came over here to look out of the window and I
couldn't resist picking up a page. It's the reporter
in me.'

This was invasion of privacy and industrial
espionage; he'd be bound to be furious and she
stiffened, expecting to be blasted. But he drawled,
'You were wasting your time; I wouldn't be leaving
anything that mattered about with a reporter in the
room.'

That was cynical but sensible, and she trotted out
the obvious excuse. 'I was worried about the
Sentinel. We all are.'

'Is that why you're here, on behalf of your
workmates? Have you come to make me an offer
for keeping the bulldozers away?'

He was laughing at her. 'No,' she said, 'I damn
well haven't. Nobody knew I was coming and
there's nothing on offer from me.' But they would
all be anxious to hear anything she might learn and
she asked, 'Are you likely to be closing us down?'

'Why should I do that?'

She had moved back almost to the table. Now they were standing facing each other and claustrophobia was something she got when she was too near him. The space around had nothing to do with it. It would probably be the same if she ran into him on the Yorkshire moors. 'No answer at all,' she said, 'And please don't say "Trust me".'

'I wouldn't dream of it.'

'Do folk trust you?' If they did, heaven help them. 'Do women?' she taunted and he retorted,

'Do men trust you?'

They always had. Even the men who fell for her never accused her of being less than honest with them. She should just say yes, instead of challenging him, 'What do you think?' because when he looked steadily at her she wanted to put up her hands and cover her face.

After a few seconds, he said, 'I think they do. You have this wide-eyed freshness about you. I should think your friends are always saying, "You can rely on Millie." But I doubt if you're quite what you seem.'

She couldn't have given herself away. She had been wary of him but he couldn't know why. 'So, what am I?' she said lightly.

'That's what I hope to find out. Come and sit down.' She turned towards her chair at the table, but he meant on the sofa and she sat down beside him reluctantly, keeping her distance. 'This is quite a place, isn't it?' she said, and she started to tell him about the last time she was here, for the engagement party.

She could hear herself chattering as though someone else was speaking, while she sat holding her breath. Her skin seemed to have become hyper-sensitive. She could feel the pressure of hands that were not touching her, his shoulder against her own as if he leaned towards her.

When he did she went on talking, although her blood was pounding in her ears, almost deafening her. And then, in slow, slow motion it seemed, he raised her face on a cupped hand and kissed her and that went straight to her heart, as fierce and piercing as a lance.

It had not been a passionate kiss, just a brushing of lips, but it scared her half to death. Her voice was still not her own but the words were still coming. 'Something I'd better make plain—I'm not available. Not for a one-night stand, not for anything. I'm heavily committed and I don't cheat.

'If I gave the wrong impression coming here I'm sorry, I should have explained before. I'm not wearing a ring and there are——' she made a small grimace '—complications, but that is how it is. Thank you for the meal. If you think I owe you for that——'

'Thank *you*. I've enjoyed your company.' He was cheerfully accepting her right to say no. 'He's a lucky man,' he said, and she nearly asked, Who is? because she was committed to nobody.

That lie was to protect herself. Other men had stirred her, she considered herself a sensuous woman, but nothing had prepared her for that surge of primitive lust just now.

Adam Schofield was her brother's enemy and so he was hers. She was never likely to forget that, but physically she had never met a man she wanted more.

CHAPTER THREE

IN THE car park Adam Schofield said goodnight
and Millie got into her car, fixing her seatbelt and
pulling out, narrowly missing a Jaguar that had
right of way to the exit. At least that jerked her
back to where she was and what she was doing. She
had managed to sound calm and collected up to
now, but nothing like this had ever happened to her
before and she had no idea how to deal with it.

Love at first sight she had heard about, of course,
but never experienced and never really believed in;
and this was light years from love. This was just
chemistry, but terrifyingly potent. If Adam had
taken her into his arms she could have gone up in
flames and it might have taken forever before her
mind got control of her body again.

Her mind wasn't doing her much good now. She
was keeping an eye on the road and driving
competently to get herself home, but all the
common sense seemed to have been knocked out
of her.

When she let herself into the house Flower nearly
knocked her over. It was his usual boisterous
welcome. She was always prepared for it and she
always fussed over him for a moment, but tonight
he sent her reeling back against the wall.

My God, she thought, my legs are giving way.
I'm falling apart.

'Is that you, dear?' her mother called from upstairs.

'Yes,' Millie called back, and thought, It looks like me, it sounds like me, but I am not at all sure that it is me.

She opened the back door and let the dog out on to the lawn that went down to the river. There was no moon in the sky and no stars. She couldn't remember a darker night.

He raced around for a few minutes then came slowly back and sat at the bottom of the stairs, watching her climb up.

There was a light on in her mother's room. Elena was in bed, turning the pages of a fashion magazine. 'Did you have a nice time?' she asked. She liked Millie to have a nice time, but it didn't displease her when Millie's relationships petered out. Elena told her friends, and herself, that she hoped Millie would find a nice man and settle for him some day. But in her heart of hearts sharing her daughter would have come almost as hard as sharing her husband, and that of course was unthinkable.

'Yes, I did,' said Millie.

'There was a phone call for you. He said he'd call again.'

'Who was it?' It wouldn't be Adam but it could be one of several others. Between steadies Millie always had somebody wanting to date her.

'He didn't say.'

'When was it?'

'About half an hour ago.'

Then it wasn't Adam, going back to the hotel and after a few minutes ringing here to ask if he could see her again. He had accepted her story of

the man in her life but he had said he'd enjoyed
her company. So perhaps he would want to go on
as friends, although he hadn't suggested that. And
if he did suggest it there was no way Millie was
agreeing.

She was undressed, just getting into bed, when
the phone rang in the hall below, and this time she
was almost certain it was Adam. There was no
glimmer of light round her mother's door now; she
had been sitting up till Millie came in, and Flower
was still sprawled at the bottom of the stairs,
although usually he slept in front of the Aga in the
kitchen.

She came down barefooted. Her hand trembled
as she reached for the phone and her, 'Hello,' was
a whisper.

'Millie,' said Jack. She hadn't wanted it to be
Adam but the relief felt like disappointment. 'Can
you talk?'

'Yes,' she went on whispering, 'she's in bed.
There's no one here.'

'How did it go?' Jack wanted a report. He had
probably phoned earlier; he seemed anxious to hear
all about it but she would rather have waited till
morning.

She said, 'We had a meal at the hotel where he's
staying. We talked, but he didn't tell me anything
incriminating about himself or anyone else.'

'You got on all right?'

'Yes.'

'Seeing him again?'

'I don't think so.' She took a deep breath. 'We
were in a private room and when he kissed me I

told him there was a man I was having this serious affair with and I didn't need another.'

'Is there?' He was surprised because she usually told him what she was doing, who she was going around with, and quite recently she had said that she was cooling off Jeremy.

'No, but it stopped the kissing.'

'Mmm.' That sounded as though he meant it was a pity about that, and she said sharply,

'What were you expecting me to do, sleep with him?'

'*No!*' He was shocked to the quick when she put it that bluntly.

'Good,' she said. 'Because I haven't had much experience in pillow-talk interviews.'

'Millie, I swear I didn't mean that, I'm sorry——'

'I'm tired,' she said. 'Let's leave it till tomorrow.'

She hung up and went back to bed. Pillow-talk was part of Jack's stock-in-trade. There had been pillow-talk in the story he had touted around about Adam Schofield, but that had cost Jack a small fortune and ever since Schofield had been his *bête noire*. 'I hate that bloody man,' he had told Millie, and that was another secret they shared, she and her half-brother who seemed nearer her twin.

She could never like Adam Schofield, but he had quickened a hunger in her like the call of the wild and she was so sure she would dream about him that she tried to stay awake as long as possible.

But keeping him out of her thoughts was exhausting, and hopeless. When she did fall into a troubled slumber she was back in the hotel, in the green-carpeted corridor. The greenness was rough deep grasses, dragging around her ankles, but she kept stumbling on because something was dragging her towards the door. In the room was a man with a scar on his face, and she still staggered forward, powerless to stop. She could feel chains or ropes that she couldn't see, pulling her; and when she reached him and his arms closed around her she was wrapped in flame and the pain woke her as she started to scream.

She thought she might have screamed. She was sitting bolt upright, her lips stretched as if she was screaming. Flower was in the room so she must have made some sound, if it was only a whimper.

She could see the shape of his great dark head against the white quilt, and she must be quiet because when she whimpered he keened. She had tried to weep privately in her bedroom when her great-aunt died last year and outside her door Flower had sat howling like a banshee.

Now she stroked his head and whispered, 'It's all right, go to sleep, everything's all right,' and he settled down on the bedside rug waiting for any further sign that she needed comforting. That night was another first for Millie. After nearly half an hour of restlessness she got up and went into the bathroom and took one of her mother's sleeping pills. Elena didn't take them regularly but she liked having a supply. She was a worrier. Any sort of stress, from getting ready for Christmas to an income tax demand, could have her saying, 'I shall have to take my pills tonight dear, I hardly closed my eyes last night.'

Millie had never taken a sleeping pill in her life, but they were low strength and one might make the difference between getting some quiet sleep and moaning and tossing and starting Flower howling.

It also made a difference in that she overslept, and woke to hear the dog barking downstairs and Amy's voice in the hall presumably taking in the post. When she looked at her clock Millie shot into the bathroom and dressed at speed and ran down the stairs and into the kitchen.

Amy came at half-past eight, Millie was due in the office at nine, and Amy was laying the table for Elena's breakfast. She gasped when she saw Millie, 'I thought you'd gone in early.'

'No, I'm late. What's that?'

That was a big bunch of long-stemmed yellow roses in the sink. Millie and her mother both got flowers sometimes. 'Who's Adam?' asked Amy.

Millie ducked her head to hide her expression, sniffing the flowers and reading the card. 'Thank you, Adam.'

'And what's he thanking you for?' Amy wanted to know.

'Not a lot,' said Millie.

'New one, isn't he?'

'Absolutely. Would you put them in water for me? I've overslept.'

She was only a few minutes late in the office, parking the car at the back of the building because she would be needing it today, and as she hurried towards the stairs the girl on Reception called, 'Enjoy yourself with the boss last night?'

'What?' Millie stopped on the bottom step. If Sally down here knew, they all knew. 'Good meal,' she said. 'They do a good meal.'

In the reporters' room, standing and sitting, they all turned to face her as she walked in and Lyn said, 'You might have said you'd got a date with Adam Schofield. I thought you said he wasn't your type.'

'Who told you?' As she asked, Millie wondered why she was asking, because the hotel had been full of staff and guests. Any of them could have recognised her and him; they had hardly met in secret.

'Somebody told Mrs Beale,' said Lyn. Mrs Beale manned the switchboard and she was better at gathering news than most of the reporters.

Lyn was Millie's closest friend here and she added resentfully, 'You could have told me.'

'Sorry about that,' Millie began to go through her drawer for the map and the notebook and the pocket recorder she would need today, explaining while not exactly lying, 'I thought he might tell me if he had any plans for the *Sentinel*, and if you'd known I was having a meal with him you'd all have been on at me, wouldn't you? Well, you are now, aren't you, and I can't tell you anything because I didn't learn a thing.'

'Now I'd have bet he could teach you plenty. Better watch out, Millie. He's the sort to have a woman in every town and it looks as if you're his bit of local colour.'

Jeremy Warrald was the sports writer with whom Millie had had a tepid affair and, looking into his jealous face, she wondered what she could ever have seen in him. She said crisply, 'I'm not his anything, any more than I was yours.'

'Stay the night, did you?' he sneered.

'Didn't Mrs Beale's informant inform you on that?'

'She said you were still in his private rooms when she went off duty.'

Somebody had been keeping tabs. Somebody was interested in Adam Schofield, which could be most of the female staff and one who was off duty before Millie had come down and gone home.

She said, 'Well, it was after nine o'clock when the trouble started.' She half covered her face with her hand as if she was embarrassed. 'He seemed a perfect gentleman up till then, when he suddenly went wild and pounced on me.'

There was an incredulous silence. 'I hit him with a candlestick,' she said, 'and he chased me along the corridors right down to the foyer.' She gave it about three seconds, scanning the faces for the scandalised and the sceptical. Then she said solemnly, 'I'm thinking of bringing charges for attempted rape,' and it dawned on them all that they were being fooled.

'Gerroff,' said one of the men and she said,

'That's what I said,' then grinned. 'No, he never laid a hand on me and of course I didn't stay the night. Sorry, it would have been more fun the other way, wouldn't it?'

Lyn hovered, when the others wandered away, to ask, 'Are you seeing him again?'

'Seeing, maybe,' said Millie. 'Dating, I doubt it. I must dash. I'm heading for the hills.'

She surprised herself sometimes, how well she could put on a flippant act. She had laughed that off so that even Lyn believed her account of last night, and it was nearly what had happened. Adam Schofield had hardly touched her. From meeting her in the foyer to seeing her into her car he had

been a charming and courteous host. And that kiss
was scarcely a touch, but it had been enough to
blow Millie's mind, so that if he had attempted rape
it would not have been rape at all.

Millie spent most of that day climbing hills, walking
alongside ditches, getting over stiles and through
closed and sometimes chained five-barred gates in
the company of the local Ramblers' Club, who were
intent on opening a public right of way that had
almost disappeared. It was not the weather for
rambling but they were determined, clad in heavy
boots and anoraks because although it was not
raining the ground was muddy from previous
downpours and most of the time a strong wind
blew.

She was not going to get much of a story out of
this. It was hardly riveting copy, not even when the
leader slipped into a waterlogged ditch. The farmers
and landowners who might have objected didn't
bother so the ramblers trudged on, and at the end
of the day they and Millie had covered over ten
weary miles. She couldn't wait to get home and into
a hot bath, especially as she had to go out again
later.

There was a car she didn't recognise in the drive
of her home. This was her mother's night for
playing bridge when one of her friends usually collected her, but not usually as early as this and never
in this kind of car.

As soon as she saw the Rolls, her first thought
was—Adam. She had thought about him a lot
today. The ramblers never stopped talking but
Millie found herself tramping on, with her head

bowed against the wind and Adam Schofield on her mind to the exclusion of almost everything else.

Seeing the car prepared her for meeting him again, and she hadn't wanted that. If she had come to any conclusion at all during her day-long hike it was that she would rather keep away from him. She had even prepared what she was going to say to Jack, when she told him that Adam Schofield had not been in touch again and she certainly was not chasing him up. If he was here she wouldn't have that excuse.

She drove past his car and left hers outside the garage, she would be needing it again later. Then she let herself in the house by the back door, she need not pass the drawing-room door that way to get to the stairs and the bathroom. She was in no state to meet anyone until she had cleaned up. She had changed her wellies for driving shoes but she was windblown and weary, and when Flower rushed her she grabbed him to hush him.

'Is that you, dear?' Elena called in clear fluting tones. 'You have a visitor.'

Give me five minutes, Millie could have called back. But if it was Adam—and she knew it was— he could think she couldn't face him without prettying herself up first.

She took off her coat, and slipped it over the post at the bottom of the stairs. There was some mail on the hall table but the sight of herself in the long oval mirror that hung over the table was enough to be dealing with right now. She ran hasty fingers over her hair, rubbed a mud smear from her cheek with the back of her hand, and tried to look at ease walking into the drawing-room.

There he was, standing by the marble fireplace, tall and elegant. And powerful. Without saying a word or making a move the power of his personality could knock you back.

She heard her mother give a little cry of dismay. 'Millie, you look as if you've been dragged through a hedge.'

'You're right there,' Millie said gaily, walking across to stand behind her mother's chair, instinctively putting a barrier between herself and the man, 'I've been out with the Ramblers, walking an old right of way. But it was a non-event because nobody stopped us.'

'That must have been frustrating,' he said.

'It was. I was hoping for somebody with a double-barrelled shotgun shouting, "They shall not pass."' She wondered if a shotgun would stop him, resenting him just walking in like this, and demanded, 'What are *you* doing here?'

'Millie,' her mother said again. She was not used to Millie sounding truculent. 'Those beautiful flowers——'

The long-stemmed roses had been arranged in an alabaster vase on a low table. Her mother would have done that, choosing a vase with delicate yellow and gold tracery that complemented the yellow blooms. Amy usually put flowers in the nearest big enough jug.

'They are beautiful,' said Millie. 'Thank you.' But she didn't sound particularly grateful and Elena gushed,

'It's been lovely meeting you; I hope you'll enjoy your stay in our little town.'

Of course Millie was uncomfortable because she looked so dishevelled. It was making her gauche in front of this sophisticated man, but there was nothing Elena could do about that and she had to get ready herself for her evening with friends.

She explained charmingly that she had to leave them, and as she closed the door behind her Millie took a step to follow and escape. 'I've got some mail in the hall,' she said. 'I'd better see what it's about.'

'Just a minute.' He came across, between her and the door, and held out a hand.

Again she moved instinctively, this time backing nearly to the wall, asking, 'Is this goodbye?'

'I hope not. Will you take my hand?'

'What for?' She was managing to sound as if she was smiling.

'I don't know.' He was not smiling. From an arm's length distance he looked down at her. 'Tell me something,' he said. 'When I kissed you, what did you feel?'

'I don't remember. Was that a kiss?' Now she sounded as if she was laughing, but when he took that step closer and she knew he was going to kiss her again all her pretences fell away. 'Don't do that,' came out in deadly earnest.

'Why not?' He still didn't touch her but she could feel his hands on her.

'I told you——' she began, and he finished,

'That you're in love with—what's his name?'

'Never you mind,' she said inanely.

'But I do mind. Do you have this effect on him?'

The closeness was terrifying. She could feel it in every nerve and he must mean that he could too. 'That's chemistry,' she said desperately.

'Is it?' he said. 'All I know is that when I kissed you last night it was as though I'd been wanting you all my life. I don't know how I managed to let you go, but I did. And then down in the car park, when you nearly hit that car, I had a split second of seeing you injured or worse and I was in hell.'

She couldn't get any further away. She had backed to the wall but she couldn't take her eyes from his face.

'I haven't been able to get you out of my mind since,' he said. She shook her head then, although it had been the same for her. He had been in her thoughts all day long.

'You feel it too, don't you.' He still didn't touch her but he traced the outline of her face, a hair's breadth away, and when he almost brushed her mouth she turned away with a soft cry that was almost a moan. 'I want you,' he said.

Other men had said that, but the words had never roused this hunger inside her as though her senses were running wild, and she went on shaking her head like something trapped.

He thought he had her. He had the cruelty of the born hunter and he was already moving in for the kill. If she had known less about him she might have been an easy prey, but he was the last man she dared give way to. 'Tell me you don't want me,' he said, and she couldn't say that. With a pulse beating in the soft hollow in her throat and blood flaming on her cheekbones, he would have known she was lying. But today she was not quite out of her mind.

She said, 'I don't want to want you.' She got up then, and walked to the roses, fiddling with the perfect arrangement for something to look at and something to do with her hands.

'It's no problem for you,' she said. 'You want and you take—what could be simpler? And I'm a healthy specimen, and I was the one who wasn't smiling and that got your attention, and now you think that sex might be something because the electricity seems to be pretty high voltage.'

She stabbed herself on a thorn and left the flowers alone. 'Chemistry, electricity, whatever,' she said. 'I admit that's there all right, but as for taking it from there, no, thank you.'

He said, 'Tell me about him.'

She was going no further with this fiction of a secret lover; even inventing a name could trip her later. 'You don't need to know anything about him.' Her voice rose, and she went from the flowers towards the door still talking, 'All that matters is that I know him well. But I don't know you at all and I've always gone by the rule—which isn't old-fashioned any more—never sleep with a stranger.'

'Then we must get to know each other.'

She had been talking her way to the door but that stopped her. Jack would love this. Adam Schofield ready and willing to tell her what he might not tell everybody. Nothing damaging, obviously, but confidential remarks could be followed up; one thing might lead to another. Jack had a network at his disposal for following clues and bringing the skeletons tumbling out of the cupboards.

He would give his eye-teeth for the kind of information she might give him, and so would she. Well, no she wouldn't, but it was an offer she could hardly refuse and she said, 'That could be interesting. No one can have too many friends.'

'It will be interesting, I guarantee.'

'And a Schofield guarantee can be relied on?' She was starting to smile. The tension had lessened now she was not being threatened any more. He thought this was the way to get her into his bed in the end but it was not. There was no way, and some time she might have to say, 'I only offered friendship; I always told you I had a lover.'

Now she said, 'I must get washed and changed.'

'Then what are you doing?'

'Eating. After that the theatre; I'm covering a play.'

'I'll come with you.'

'I shouldn't think amateur dramatics are for you.'

He gave her his quizzical look. 'But—apart from yourself—you don't know what's for me, do you? I shall watch you at work and I shall read your write-up.'

'You wouldn't be thinking of censoring me? I couldn't be doing with that. I'm an old hand at this, and what experience have you had reviewing amateur dramatics?' Of course he wouldn't; she was fooling.

'Never mind about experience,' he said, 'it's my newspaper, I'm the boss and a little professional deference wouldn't come amiss.'

'Deference, he wants,' she jeered. And gets, she thought; but for the moment I am privileged. I can be as sharp as I like so long as I keep my claws sheathed.

She scooped up the envelopes, one large two small, from the hall table and took them upstairs with her. As she passed her mother's open bedroom door Elena signalled her in to mouth, 'He's still here?'

'Yes, we're going to the theatre.'

Her mother was sitting at the dressing-table, putting the final touches to her make-up with a mascara wand. She squinted at her own reflection while Millie stood just inside the doorway. 'He's very handsome, of course. And very rich, I suppose. He *is* the man who's bought the *Sentinel*?'

She knew he was. As soon as he told her his name she would have asked him that.

'That's the one,' said Millie.

'I didn't know you knew him.' When she put down the mascara wand Elena looked at Millie's reflection.

'He came round the office.'

'And picked you out?' That surprised her mother.

'I suppose so.'

'And sent you flowers. That's very romantic but—well, do be careful dear. He's a man of the world; he could go to a girl's head.'

Usually Elena treated her daughter as if Millie was older than she was, relying on her in all sorts of ways. But occasionally her mind did a backward leap, making Millie sixteen or so again, like tonight.

We've come to an arrangement, Millie could have said. He isn't going to seduce me until I'm good and ready, and I'm never going to be ready. So that's all right, isn't it, because that's what you're bothered about.

She smiled and said, 'It is all right, I do know what I'm doing.'

She hoped she did, but there was no time to start wondering. As soon as she got into her room she opened the big envelope first. The address was typewritten and inside was a blue folder that fell open as she took it out, scattering its contents at her feet. A photograph of Adam Schofield with a woman and a man looked up at her.

It was a dossier from Jack. Schofield's CV and a mass of background information, and she gathered up the photocopied pages with a quick glance at each before she put the folder away in a drawer.

She would read and remember this, because the more she knew about him the easier it should be to get on with him, and then she would get rid of it. Nobody was going to find it up here but she could have spilled the pages and the photograph in front of him downstairs, and that made it seem like dynamite.

They ate curry, in a local restaurant that prided itself on genuine Indian cuisine, with red and gold flock wallpaper and brass lamps swinging from the ceiling. It was a popular place, almost full although this was early evening, and Millie tucked into a mild, creamy prawn korma while Adam chose a hotter madras.

They talked food. Making a joke of their getting to know each other, Millie was doing a spoof interview on his likes and dislikes—although even that was covered in Jack's dossier—when a man who had just come into the restaurant stopped at their table and said '*Adam*!'

Then he recognised Millie and said, 'Hello' to her, but it was Schofield he was pleased to see and Adam greeted him like an old friend.

David Forrest was a local businessman who had once, very briefly, almost been a politician. He was a pleasant-faced man, built like a rugby player, and his wife, with him, had a sweet smile.

They stayed long enough for Adam to ask how they and the children were doing and to be told everything was fine.

'Come and have dinner with us,' Rosemary Forrest urged. 'Any night; we'd love to have you. You too,' she included Millie. 'We'd love to have both of you.'

'Thank you,' said Adam. 'We'll be in touch.'

'Thank you very much,' Millie murmured, although that was one invitation she couldn't accept. She had pitied David Forrest's wife, but if the facts were known Rosemary Forrest would never let Millie Hands into her home.

'Friends of yours?' she asked as they were ushered to their table. It was a silly question but he said,

'I've known them for some time. I suppose you have too.'

Millie had known of them. David Forrest owned an engineering works and she had interviewed him in the run-up to last year's by-election.

'Quite a while,' she said and speared a prawn in her curry. 'He was nearly your MP.'

'That was a bad business. He's a good bloke; he'd have made a good MP.'

David Forrest's downfall had been a gorgeous but not very successful model with whom he had once spent a weekend. Millie had heard a rumour after he was selected as candidate and passed it on to Jack. Jack's contacts had tracked the girl down and, for a sizeable sum, she had relived her fling as 'I was a sex slave' for three lurid weeks in a Sunday tabloid.

Before the last edition came out, Forrest stood down. Every word was devoured locally, although it was the kind of story the *Sentinel* would never have published, except to report that for personal reasons David Forrest would not be standing and describe the happy home life of the man who would.

He was Millie's most flamboyant exposé but not her only one. She had given Jack several tips for scoops. She loathed hypocrites. The men—they were nearly always men—who thought they could smile and get away with murder. She had no sympathy for David Forrest and she said now, 'It *was* a bad business, but don't you think there are enough cheats in Parliament?'

She must not start arguing this way or she could get heated and she must stay cool. She forced a smiling grimace, 'And everywhere else, I'm sure; there's a lot of it about. About this play we're going to see. Perhaps I should warn you; they're a very arty company, none of your cheap and cheerful about them. Have you heard of *The Changeling*?'

'Who's he?'

'That's the play. It's a Jacobean tragedy of lust, murder and madness.'

'I can see we're in for a night to remember,' he said solemnly.

The Players did consider themselves a cut above the average dramatics society. The plays they chose were always heavy and Millie had taken a copy of tonight's from the county library to get an idea what she was in for. Although it sounded just right for the Players it was not something Millie would have paid her own money to see. But this was work and all the members of the company could act. They took themselves very seriously indeed, and always put on an impressive show.

The Playhouse had once been a barn, turned into an intimate little theatre by two opera singers, husband and wife, both semi-retired and putting on these shows two or three times a year.

Millie was welcomed as Press. The *Sentinel* always gave glowing reviews. But having Adam Schofield with her got her VIP treatment, and a suppressed fit of the giggles at the warmth of the invitation to join the get-together afterwards.

She usually went over to the house when the performance was over, to chat with the cast, but tonight every Player this side the curtain seemed to want her to promise not to hurry away.

'You're very popular,' Adam said when they reached their seats and she smiled,

'It's you they want over there.'

'You're the critic.'

'Yes, but I never give them a bad review. You're the man the men think has clout.' She rolled her eyes. 'And the women think you could do nicely.'

'Do what nicely?'

She laughed at his wicked grin. 'Well, they're not going to ask you to join the company.' He did look and sound as if he might make an actor but the women wanted him around because he was the most striking man to walk in here tonight.

'Do we join them afterwards?' she asked.

'Let's get through the play first.'

The curtain rose on a girl praying and Millie, knowing the plot, knew that she was due for rape and destruction before the final curtain. She was to be pursued by a man she disliked and feared who was to possess her in the end, body and soul.

When De Flores first stepped forward to face Beatrice Millie gasped because the actor had disfigured himself with a livid scar running down his cheek. Adam turned to ask quietly, 'Anything the matter?'

'No,' she whispered back. 'Only I dreamt of you last night and you had a scar.' She hadn't meant to tell him and she smiled as if it was amusing.

'I dreamt of you,' he said, 'and you had no scar.'

She didn't believe that. He had said he couldn't get her out of his mind but she was sure she had never disturbed his sleep and she was wishing he had not come here with her. If she had been alone, or with somebody else, she would have thought this was a steamy saga. A bit over the top perhaps, with the Players hurling themselves into their blood and thunder roles. But there were lines that made her shudder.

'I'll haunt her still. If I get nothing else I'll have my will,' from the dark man with the scarred face. And the girl . . . 'I think of some harm towards me. Danger is in my mind . . .'

It was all make-believe, of course but, with Adam Schofield close beside her in the darkened theatre the grim story became real enough at times to chill

Millie's blood. When Beatrice moaned, 'I'm forced to love thee now,' with De Flores' dagger at her heart and his own, Millie felt a wave of sickness that was not all due to the rich curry and the stuffiness of the little theatre.

When the play ended and the corpses got up to take their bows Adam said, 'Powerful stuff.'

Millie said 'Wow!' clapping heartily because it had been a good production.

She had no choice about joining the company afterwards. She was grabbed as they moved out of their seats and there was a buffet laid out in the drawing-room of the big old house adjoining the barn.

This was one of the Players' traditions, this supper after the show, with the actors still in costumes and make-up entertaining the friends they had invited.

Millie knew most of them. She introduced Adam around and he said all the right things, discussing and praising their performances so that he was leaving all of them glowing.

The actor with the scar was less sinister this side of the footlights, where the scar was obviously greasepaint and his dark wig had slid up his forehead. Millie told everybody how much she had enjoyed the play, and she had eaten a large cream meringue before she realised that was not a good idea.

'Let's go,' Adam said quietly at her elbow, and she began to make excuses about an early start in the morning. They were followed to Adam's car by several of the company, including their hostess, a large lady in purple plush, who seemed reluctant to let them go, and very impressed by the Rolls, Millie found herself smiling and waving goodbye through the car window like minor royalty.

'I've never been seen to my car by Maud before,' she said. 'Very grand, is Maud. She was an opera singer.'

He turned the car out on to the road. It went so smoothly, headlights cutting through the darkness. 'So she said,' he said. 'She was offering to sing for me,' and Millie gurgled,

'So that's why we got out.'

There was a grand piano in the drawing-room and she could picture Maud, accompanied by a pianist, standing there and belting out something very loud and passionate at Adam. 'You don't know what you missed,' she said. 'Maud can shatter wine glasses.'

He winced. 'Thanks for warning me. What are you saying in your write-up?'

'They were good. They're mad for culture but they're very professional.' She should not have eaten that cream cake. A slight sickly headache was making her frown but she went on, 'Well, I thought they were good.'

'They were,' he agreed. 'Nearly professional.'

'I'd say very.' She was arguing for arguing's sake. She had done a lot of smiling tonight and she was beginning to feel the strain. When he enquired lightly,

'Do you see everything through rose-coloured spectacles?' she snapped,

'No, I do not.'

'How about this lover of yours?'

'I know him through and through. I see him as he is.' As there was no such man she couldn't see him at all, and she was not spinning any more fantasies or Adam would trip her before long, she was sure of that.

'And how do you see me?' he asked, which did at least change the subject.

She might have told him what she saw and knew when she looked at him but of course she couldn't. His profile against the dark window glass was clean and hard, and another of Beatrice's lines from that damn play came into her head. '"When we are used to a hard face it is not so displeasing,"' she said, and he caught her hand and lifted it to his lips and quoted De Flores.

'"Her fingers touched me; she smells all amber."'

She felt the touch run through her and babbled, 'How does amber smell?'

'Like peaches, hot sun on sand, burnt toast.'

'That's me,' she said. 'Especially the burnt toast.'

Flower started barking as their car drew up in front of the house and she said, 'All right, all right, I'm coming, I'll take you for a walk, just don't rouse the neighbourhood.'

'Where are you walking him?'

The slight headache was still with her; fresh air would do her good. 'The usual,' she said. 'Along the river for a little way.'

'That's my way.'

'Are you on the boat?'

'Yes. Come and have a coffee.'

She didn't think so but she opened the front door and Flower bounded out, and they left the car and walked round the house across the lawn to the towpath.

All her life Millie had loved everything about the river. She had played along here as a child, walked the banks in fair and foul weather, and for the last four years with her great dog beside her. Usually Flower ranged the meadows but in darkness he kept more or less at Millie's heels.

They didn't do much talking. She told Adam about some of the Players he had just met, how Maud and Maurice had converted the barn, but mostly they walked in silences that were filled with the gentle lapping of water against the banks, dogs barking in the distance and Flower answering back, the hooting of an owl and the cry of a night creature.

When they neared her boat and the little bridge to the island she asked, 'May I use your bathroom? Cream on top of curry seems to have disagreed with me.'

This time she avoided the mud, stepping off the bridge on to the deck, following him down the steps and through the galley into the saloon.

As he stopped to light a lamp she went down to the other end, through the bunkroom into the bathroom. She was a few minutes in there, using the loo and undecided whether she was going to be sick, but after she had washed her hands and bathed her face she began to feel better.

It was eating nothing all day. Getting up too late for breakfast and saying no, thank you to the ramblers' offers of sandwiches. Then a rich curry and finally—she still couldn't bear to think about the meringue stuffed with cream.

Now she would go home, and there was no need for Adam to walk with her and then have to return. She hoped Flower would be as good as a body-guard in an emergency, although so far he had never had to prove it.

As she went through the bunkroom she stumbled over a boot and stopped to look around. Then she came round the dresser-divider into the saloon. He had two lamps burning now and they cast a mellow glow over everything. 'Someone's been sleeping in your bed,' she said. 'But don't get excited, it isn't Goldilocks.'

'What?'

There was enough light coming through the porthole and from the lamps to see the figure, sleeping peacefully on the bunk. Al, coming back from the pub, must have forgotten he'd moved. Either the door was open or he still had a key. Anyhow he was here now and Adam swore softly.

'What are you going to do?' Millie asked.

'Sling him out.'

'Where? He can't sleep on the floor, he's got old bones.'

'If he can't find his way to his lodgings I was thinking of the riverbank.'

She wasn't sure if he meant that. 'Shame on you,' she said. 'That's downright vindictive.'

'And how charitable would you feel if he was between your sheets?'

'You've got a point.' There was a spare bedroom at home but she dared not put Adam Schofield in that. 'I could offer you a bunk on the *Sandpiper*,' she said, 'but it is rather cramped and everything's battened down.'

'Would you be sharing it with me?'

'*No!*'

He grinned, 'Then it's back to the hotel. I'll leave a note for the homing pigeon here.'

'More a cuckoo in the nest,' said Millie.

Al grunted, rolled and stretched, enjoying a well deserved night's sleep, and looking down at him Adam said, 'I'd like to get him by the scruff of the neck and dump him in the bloody river.'

If she had not been here Millie felt that Al would have been frogmarched off the boat. When he woke he was going to kick himself, because his only excuse was no excuse at all. Adam had written on the back of an envelope, 'You should have vacated this boat. Schofield.' Then he shook his head, starting to laugh,

'Is this likely to happen again? Resident ghosts I can stand, but this one is too solid by half. I don't need him coming out of the woodwork.'

She was glad he was laughing. 'It must be over thirty years he's been coming home to this boat. Hard to break that long a habit.'

'He'll break it after I've seen him tomorrow.' She didn't envy Al that interview and she pleaded,

'Go easy with him. He's a very kind, caring man.'

'You and your rose-coloured spectacles.'

Suddenly Al snored, a rasping intake of breath ending in a full-throated roar that had Flower growling and Millie giggling. 'You'll know if he's about,' she said. 'I'll give you a key to the *Sandpiper*; next time you can roll him in there.' There wouldn't be a next time. Al wouldn't be this daft twice.

Walking her home Adam asked, 'How long have you had your boat?'

'Just over a year.'

'Do you sail alone?'

'Usually. Only on the rivers but it's my little kingdom. My island with no bridges.'

'I know what you mean,' he said. 'I bought a lighthouse.'

'You did?' That was something she hadn't known, although it might be in Jack's dossier. 'Where is it?'

'In Cornwall. On the rocks below the house.'

She knew about the house but she said, 'Tell me about it,' and he described the home that had once been an abbey, on the rugged coastline with the rocks and the shining sands and the stormy seas crashing over.

'There are times when you can't beat a lighthouse for isolation,' he said, and she wished this were more what it seemed, that he were someone she could let herself care about.

She waited for him to get into his car, and as he turned the key in the door he said, 'I have to go back for a few days next week. Will you come with me?'

'I can't do that.'

'Why not?'

She had days off owing and he was the boss at work. Her mother could manage with Amy and Ben. But going away with Adam Schofield would be madness.

He was smiling at her. 'It's a big house. Your own room, of course, and plenty of people around.

You say you want to know more about me—well, here's your chance: the keys to the castle.'

She made herself smile too. She was tired now, from the ten-mile hike as well as the curry and cream, and forced gaiety was getting harder. 'I hope they haven't let your rooms at the hotel,' she said.

'If they have they'll find me others.'

'I'm sure they will. Sleep well.'

'You too, and don't dream of men with scars.'

He got into the car and closed the door and she blinked, half expecting to see a scarlet line on the smooth dark face that turned towards her for a moment before he drove away.

'Is that you, dear?' her mother called as Millie and Flower went into the hall.

'Yes, *yes*,' Millie called back.

There was another car outside. Whoever had brought her mother home from her bridge evening was in the drawing-room with her, but Millie didn't feel up to putting her head round the door and saying goodnight. She was wrung out, ready to fall into bed, but she should phone Jack and tell him the dossier had arrived. And that she did not want to go on with this. She had not realised what havoc it would play with her.

Flower padded upstairs close behind her. If she closed her bedroom door on him he could start howling outside so she said, 'Come in and shut up; I don't want you telling everybody I'm falling apart.'

Jack answered almost at once and said, 'I was going to ring you.' There was an affinity between them. Even on the phone they often finished each other's sentences, came out with the same words, and on their rare meetings they always seemed to be in tune with each other.

Jack was brash and pushy but that was his line of business and Millie had never lacked spirit herself. Hearing his voice now, she wished she could see him. It was over six months since they had last met in London and she said, 'We ought to get together.'

'Sure,' he said. 'When and where?'

They would have to check dates and schedules. In the meantime she had to tell him what was happening here. 'I got the file,' she said. 'There's a mass of detail there. You've been doing a lot of research on him.'

'Yeah,' said Jack. 'How's it going? Have you seen any more of him?'

'He was with me when I got home tonight. He went to the theatre with me.'

'That can't be bad.' He sounded as if it was very good. He chuckled. 'How did you enjoy the show?'

'It was heavy.'

'What did you talk about? What did he say?'

...He said 'I want you.' He said, 'Her fingers touched me, she smells all amber'...

'He's asked me to go down to the house in Cornwall next week, but——' Her brother gave a whoop of triumph.

'You are a star. You're a little diamond.'

'I'm not going.'

'Ah!' He took a few seconds on that. 'You wouldn't be alone with him down there.'

'He said there'd be others, but how did you know?'

'He's going down for a wedding. Some of the guests will be staying in his house.'

'You know a lot.'

'I don't know enough. I don't know what I need to know. I need a spy in that camp like I need my right arm.'

He had to be exaggerating madly. 'Don't get paranoid,' she said.

He said, 'Listen to me Millie,' as if she was doing anything else. 'I'm not asking you to sleep with the man, you know I'm not, I'd kill him sooner. But you could keep a relationship on the edge. He's taken with you, he trusts you, and the house will be full of his friends and his business mates. You'd be mixing with them, you'd be hearing things.

'I'm not paranoid about him but I think he is about me, because he's been gunning for me for months and unless I get hold of something I can use against him he's going to put me behind bars.'

CHAPTER FOUR

'WHAT do you *mean*? What can he *do*?' Millie knew her brother was bitter about Adam Schofield but she had no idea that Schofield might still be threatening Jack. 'What's it about?' she croaked.

'Money,' Jack said bluntly. 'You've got to have money to put around in my line, and the way I got this was slightly dodgy. Put in a nutshell, Schofield has hold of something that could send me down.'

She had to gulp before she could whisper, 'To prison?'

'Yup.' He sounded almost jaunty but she was not fooled.

'Oh, God!' This was awful. 'What do you want me to do? Look for the papers?' She was sounding shrill. The last time she had gone through Adam's papers he could have caught her red-handed through something as silly as a strawberry thumbprint, and the thought of rifling his desk or trying to open a wall safe terrified her.

Jack said, 'I want you to keep your eyes and ears open for anything I can use against him.'

Downstairs in the hall she could hear her mother saying goodnight, and then the front door closing. 'I'll call you tomorrow,' she said. 'Let me think,' and she switched off the phone as Elena called,

'Millie.'

She would be wanting to know how the evening had gone, she would be coming up here now, and

Millie had only a few seconds to compose herself.
Her head was ringing but she slowed down her
breathing and tried to calm down. There had been
dishonesty, obviously, but Jack was her brother and
she seemed closer to him for the secrecy that
involved. The way she felt about Adam Schofield
was the black magic of sex that could end as ab-
ruptly as it had begun, while Jack was her blood
brother for ever.

Elena came into the room, smiling and asking,
'How was the play?'

'You know the Players.' Millie got that just right,
smiling too, and Elena—who had sat through some
of their productions—made a small grimace.

'Did Maud sing?'

'There wasn't any singing in it, thank goodness.
She did offer to sing for Adam afterwards but he
remembered he had to leave suddenly.'

Elena laughed, 'I like that. I liked him. Are you
seeing him again?' She seemed to have decided that
Millie was safe with Adam Schofield after all, but
when Millie said,

'He has to go home to Cornwall next week, he's
asked me to go with him,' Elena's eyes went wide
and apprehensive. Millie always knew what her
mother was thinking. Elena was transparent. It was
Millie who wore the mask. Now Millie said, 'The
house will be full of guests; he's going down for a
wedding.'

Adam hadn't told her that, Jack had. She must
not tell anyone else and she mustn't let her mother
repeat it in front of Adam. But it reassured Elena
who asked, after a few seconds, 'What
will you wear?'

'I don't know. I don't know if I'm going yet. Don't say anything to anyone.'

'Of course not.' Elena put on a soul-of-discretion face. 'Our secret.' And Millie, reflecting on how much of her life was a tight-shut book, murmured,

'A very little secret,' then changed the subject and asked, 'Did you have a good evening with the bridge brigade?'

'Not as much fun as you had,' her mother said gaily, 'but you're only young once,' and Millie thought, In the next week or so I could age ten years the way I'm going on, and none of it is likely to be fun.

The phone rang in the hall about half an hour later, just after she had taken in her mother's bedtime hot milk. It was Jack, apologising. 'I couldn't leave it like this. I shouldn't have landed my troubles on you like that.'

'Are things so bad?' She was hoping he had exaggerated but when he said,

'Couldn't be much worse,' that hope faded.

'I might not come up with anything,' she said. 'But I will go, I'll do all I can,' and Jack reassured her eagerly.

'I wouldn't have let you if you were going to be alone with him down there, but the house will be full. And it doesn't follow there'd be a fuss about anything you found out. A hint might do—anything that might hold him off.'

'I'll try,' she said again, and her brother said,

'I knew you would, because there's nothing I wouldn't do for you, Millie.' She knew that, just as surely as she had known that she had no choice.

'Who was that on the phone?' her mother called as Millie went past her bedroom door.

'It was work,' Millie called back. 'Just something I have to do.'

When she got into bed herself she opened the dossier that had come in this morning's mail, because this was a job of work and she must do her homework. Before interviewing anyone she always read up everything she could find about them and this file was well researched. Jack and his staff had gone to town on Adam Schofield, producing not only a biography but notes on his friends and colleagues, and details ranging from paintings he had bought to the names of his clubs.

Somebody reading this could pass themselves off as having similar tastes but nothing went beneath the surface. She had been nearer to him when he lifted her fingers to his lips, in the dark car after the play; even when they were laughing together over Al snoring in Adam's bed.

It would be useful, of course it would, but he was a complex man, and if she ever did get past his deep reserve she might find just how dangerous he was. Discovering what Adam Schofield was capable of doing could be like walking into a minefield.

The photograph was a cutting from a glossy magazine, a charity ball, Adam with a man in horn-rimmed spectacles and a fair-haired girl. The date was nearly three years ago, and the man was a Peter Barkin, of Schofield Enterprises. The girl, who was looking up at Adam, displaying a perfect profile, was actress Sharon Ward.

Millie knew about her. That trouble had hit Jack about the same time as his mother's death. He said that finding Millie was the saving of him after the grief of that and Adam Schofield nearly bankrupting him. It had been a black year, but finding his sister had played a big part in his survival. And now she was helping him to survive again.

Why couldn't Adam Schofield leave Jack alone? The out-of-court settlement should have satisfied him, although other friends of his might have fallen foul of Jack's activities since. David Forrest for one. She had started that exposé and lined up a few more. If Adam knew that he might be gunning for her too. It was not a comforting thought to go to sleep on and she sighed deeply, getting an answering whimper from Flower.

She had meant to leave the dog in the kitchen, but with this maddening instinct of his he had followed her back into her room and stretched out beside her bed. If it was at all possible she took him with her when she went away, but this time she would have to ask Ben to walk him, because she couldn't have an animal in Adam Schofield's house, howling whenever it sensed she was worried or depressed.

'You've just done yourself out of a seaside holiday,' she said, and switched off her bedside lamp and tried to relax. But she fell asleep late and woke early. Once she woke there was no sleeping again, and it was light enough to shower and dress and go downstairs into the kitchen to make herself an instant coffee.

Then she walked Flower along the riverbank towards the islet and the narrowboat. She wanted to catch Al before he left for the office. It would be grim for him, waking in Adam's bed and realising he was a squatter here. And the note was waiting, so there was no chance that the new boss hadn't come and found him snoring his head off.

Maybe Al was still sleeping; he had looked set for a long night's repose when they had left him last night. If he was she would have to wake him, and then she could tell him that Adam had seen the funny side and this was no great drama, but he had better get it into his head that the narrowboat was his home no longer.

It made her smile, remembering, and when they crossed the little bridge she called to the dog, 'Heel, and keep out of the mud.'

She tapped on the door, waiting a few moments then opened it. Through the open galley door she could see Al sitting at the end of the long saloon, his head in his hands.

'Good morning,' she called.

'Is it?' He raised his head and looked at her blearily. 'Surprised to find me here?'

'No, I came round last night.'

'Lateish?' She nodded. 'With him?'

She nodded again and asked, 'How did you get in?'

'I must have a key.' He fumbled in the pockets of his jacket, came up with a key and looked at it as though it was a surprise.

'I should hand that over if I were you,' she said.

'I thought I had. Seems I had forgotten this one.' She began to laugh and he said reproachfully, 'It isn't funny, Millie. I've made a ruddy mug of myself.'

'He thought it was funny. Honestly. He just went back to the hotel. Don't go in grinning, but I'm sure that a simple "Sorry and here's your key" should do it.'

Al puffed out his cheeks in doubt, then asked, 'You think so?'

'I'm sure of it.'

'Millie——' Something else had occurred to Al. 'Why were you coming back here with him lateish?'

'He'd been to the theatre with me and I was walking the dog.'

Dear old Al with his fatherly concern for her. He had been her father's friend but Al knew nothing of Colin Hands' affair with Jack's mother. Listening to all Al's reminiscences of her father over the years had convinced her of that.

'Schofield's a hard man,' said Alf. 'You want to watch yourself with him.'

Here she was, protecting her mother and Al, and they both thought they were looking out for her, as if she were still sixteen. She said, 'I'm a big girl now, and I'd better be taking this dog home.' Flower wagged his tail when she put a hand on him. 'A shame the stove's out and coffee isn't still brewing.'

Al grinned sheepishly, 'It wasn't till I tried to pour myself a cup that I knew something was wrong. Then I saw that note.'

'You won't do it again, will you? The door might be left open, I don't know, but don't stroll in here again, Al, much less fall into bed.'

Al shook his head vigorously, then winced and rubbed the frown between his grizzled brows, 'No danger of that. He might let this pass. He might even have got a laugh out of it. But I tell you, Millie love, he could scare the hell out of me.'

He scares you, thought Millie, and you only forgot you should have moved out of here yesterday. If you knew what I was planning to do to him you would think I was out of my mind.

'See you in the office,' she said, 'but make yourself some coffee first.' There was a Calor gas stove in the galley, and Al looked as if he needed something to get him into a fit state to face the world and Adam Schofield.

When she got back home with Flower her mother was sitting at the kitchen table drinking lemon tea. Amy was by the toaster, waiting for the bread to jump up, and as Millie walked in with the dog Elena cried, 'Down, boy,' drawing back the long full skirt of her harebell-blue velvet dressing gown.

'He isn't too bad this morning.' Millie went down on her knees to dry off his feet with a rough towel and Amy said,

'Hear you're off to a wedding in Cornwall with this chap who sent you the roses.'

Millie jumped up and turned on Elena. 'I told you not to talk about it. I haven't decided whether to go.'

'Oh, you'll go, and telling Amy isn't talking about it,' said Elena airily. Amy wouldn't gossip, but Millie wished she hadn't mentioned the wedding to her mother; she wished she hadn't told her anything yet. This must go no further until she could get the information from another source than Jack.

She looked up at the number of Alderton Towers and asked if Mr Schofield had booked in last night. Adam Schofield. The woman who answered didn't need to check. He had and he was here, now she would put through the call.

Millie waited, and when he said his name she could almost see him. Up till now her brother had been the only one who came so vividly into her mind during a telephone call, and that was always comforting even when the talking was troubled.

But when she heard 'Schofield here,' she could smell the clean tang of his aftershave although she hadn't known that she had noticed it before. She could feel his fingers on her jawbone, hard, almost hurting, lifting her face so that he could look into her eyes.

'It's Millie,' she said, and she closed her eyes as if that would hide something from him.

'I hoped it was.'

She drew a deep breath and babbled, 'About going down to Cornwall—what would we be doing there?' She knew he smiled and she rushed on, 'I mean, would we be sailing? It's rough weather for sailing. What kind of clothes would I need?'

'You're coming,' he said. 'Good.'

'Maybe. Who else would be there?'

'In the house I've got other guests staying, ten of them in all.' There should be safety in a number like that, and there would probably be other women who fancied him to take the heat off Millie... 'They're down for a wedding, a neighbour I've known all my life.'

Now he had told her, that was covered, but she said, 'I couldn't gatecrash a wedding.'

'You wouldn't be gatecrashing.' She didn't want
to go. She had to but she was very uneasy about
it, and after a few seconds' silence he asked, 'Do
you have a hang-up about weddings? Is this lover
of yours married?'

She had stammered, 'No' before she realised that
if she had said yes it would have explained the
'complications'.

'So you'll come?' he said.

'Yes.'

'I'll collect you Tuesday morning.' She had to
listen to the arrangements although she was feeling
fuzzy-headed. 'The wedding's on Wednesday and
I have to be in London Friday night. I'm there for
the weekend but I could get you back here on
Friday.' He paused and she said,

'Yes,' again.

'I'll be away from here until Tuesday so I won't
see you till then, but you will come? You will be
packed and ready, say nine o'clock?'

'Yes.' She was beginning to feel like one of those
nodding dogs in the back windows of cars and she
got a little gaiety into her voice, 'I'll be ready and
if I'm going to a wedding I'll pack a pretty hat.'
Her one pretty hat was rather battered but she might
buy another.

'You won't need a pretty hat. You'd knock them
sideways in jeans and sweater.'

She smiled at that and asked, 'Are you leaving
now?'

'In half an hour or so.'

'Will you see Al before you go?'

'No.'

'Well, I've just seen him, I walked along to the narrowboat with Flower, and he's very worried. He had the shock of his life waking up in your sheets. I think he's had enough; could we forget the whole thing?'

'Sure,' he said. 'How did he get in?'

'There was another key he'd forgotten he'd got.'

'Well, get it off him, will you?'

'I'll do that. Although,' she teased, 'if you're going to be away all next week can I tell him he can move back for a few days?'

'No, you can't. If he's still hankering for a life afloat, put him on the *Sandpiper*.'

She laughed. 'See you on Tuesday. And—just friends?'

'One more in a houseful of them.'

'That's all right then.' She hung up, smiling, wondering why she was suddenly light-hearted and realising it was because she had four days' reprieve. His voice on the phone was disturbing enough but, away from him, she could cope. She would use the time to get herself together and by Tuesday she could be in control.

First she had to arrange to take most of next week off, and that was made a little easier because when she went in to see the editor he already knew. Adam had phoned him and requested leave of absence for her and the editor was falling over himself to oblige the new owner.

So of course Millie could take the days off that were owing to her and John Adams hoped she would enjoy her break. She thanked him and as she turned away from his desk he said, 'Millie—er—

you won't get your hopes too high over this, will you? Adam Schofield—well——'

Millie smiled at John—she hoped reassuringly—and went into the reporters' room to find that her colleagues there knew too, because Mrs Beale on the switchboard had listened to every word of Schofield's phone call.

They were all surprised. Millie was a smashing girl. She was smart, and pretty enough to catch any man's eye and it wasn't surprising that Schofield fancied her. But taking her down to his home to meet his friends and accompany him to this wedding put a different slant on the situation. For the time being our Millie seemed to have hooked a very big fish, although there was no question of her landing it and they were all agreed that the fish was a shark.

But the women envied her and the men envied him, and she got warnings and congratulations in about equal numbers. 'Find out what's happening about the *Sentinel*,' she was urged, and Al handed over the key to the boat, looking gloomy. Al was not happy for her. He thought it would end in tears sooner rather than later and that all the tears would be Millie's.

She shied away from the questions they tried to ask her, offending some of the girls who said this wasn't like her at all. Millie had always been so open about everything. Not this time, thought Millie. Not for a long time...

They discussed it behind her back, because it was more interesting than most of the news they were printing, and she didn't sit around in the office much. She concentrated on work, and after work her evenings were busy. She was keeping Adam

Schofield out of her mind reasonably well. He no longer obsessed her. By Monday she could go a whole hour without thinking about him once, and when she saw him tomorrow she would still be physically attracted to him, she was prepared for that, but she should have built up a resistance against the full force of his power over her.

She had phoned Jack and told him when she was leaving and that she would be home again on Friday and he said, 'You were right, it's time we did get together.'

After this week she would need to see her brother. She asked, 'Where?'

'Can you get up here over the weekend?'

'Not London. That's where Adam will be.'

Jack laughed indulgently. 'It's a big city, we're not going to bump into him.'

'I'm not so sure about that. But he won't be here so how about the *Sandpiper*? She's still at the same mooring.'

As soon as she bought her boat Millie had been eager to show it to Jack, and they had gone upriver on a Sunday afternoon and talked of cruising together some time. That hadn't happened but it might some day. At this time of year the little boat, moored on the riverbank, was a private place where they could meet and talk and she could get a meal together.

It was settled that Jack would drive down next Sunday afternoon and she would be waiting for him in the *Sandpiper*; and on Monday, after work, she walked along the river with Flower, opening up the boat, seeing what food she had in the stern locker.

Across the water the narrowboat lay still and
silent under the willows. She missed seeing smoke
rising from the tiny chimney, being able to run
across the bridge for a cup of Al's killer coffee.

In the morning Adam would be coming for her,
and it was crazy to feel as if this was her last chance
of freedom because tomorrow she would be his
prisoner. But she found herself checking the gas
and fuel as if she were planning to unravel the
mooring ropes and sail upriver beyond the town
lock, and the next and the next, slipping away fast
and quietly from everything that was causing such
turmoil in her life.

But if she did sail away she would have to come
back. She would need more than a seven-
horsepower cabin cruiser to escape from Adam
Schofield. No wonder Jack had laughed when she
had said that London wasn't big enough to hide
from him. What was the line from the play? 'I'll
haunt her still'...

It was cold in here. It was cold everywhere. The
weather was grim, and why had the bride chosen
to get married in Cornwall in late November? There
could well be a hurricane blowing down there. Millie
came out of the boat, and locked up behind her,
and went back home to finish her packing.

She was waiting next morning. Her mother had
joined her for breakfast and Millie had made herself
swallow cereal and some toast, finally escaping back
to her bedroom and pacing up and down on the
carpet. Flower paced with her, due to start whining
any minute, so that it would be almost a relief to
get away.

When she heard the car draw up and her mother, who had been standing at a window, called, 'Millie, he's here,' it wasn't a relief at all, but she hurried. If she hadn't she might have found she couldn't move. She ran downstairs, clutching her handbag and grabbing her case, kissed her mother and said,

'Don't let Flower out or he could be chasing the car.'

Adam was just getting out of the car and he came to meet her as she began to chatter, 'Let's go. I'm leaving Flower; would you have minded if I'd brought him?'

'Not at all.'

'Well my mother will feel safer with him on guard.' That was true. That was what Elena had said, although she had a neighbour staying overnight with her while Millie was away. 'Have you had a good business trip? Was it a business trip?'

'It was, and it went well.'

'That's good.' He had taken the case from her. Her mother was waving from the window and she waved back. As she got into the car she could hear the dog barking and she twisted her hands together.

'What's the matter?' Adam asked.

'Nothing.' Oh, *hell*, she thought, I still want him to put his arms round me . . . If her fingers had not been tightly gripped she would not have been able to resist touching his face, stroking the cool firm skin. The need to get close almost overwhelmed her, as if they were lovers meeting again after a long parting.

The car drew away from the house, through the streets of the town, and she knew that he was waiting for her to speak although he kept his eyes on the road. She said, 'I shouldn't be here.'

He still waited. She said lightly, 'I've been warned against taking off with you. Some of them were quite shocked,' but she got no answering smile.

'Scandalmongering isn't bothering you,' he said. Of course it wasn't. He glanced down at her right hand. 'Nice ring.'

'Thank you.'

'For what? I didn't give it to you.' It was an antique bar of small square-cut emeralds and seed pearls. She managed to look smug and he said, 'I see. Well he's got good taste, this man of yours,' and she nodded, because that was why she was wearing the ring.

It was the only valuable piece of jewellery she had and she was passing it off as a gift from her secret lover, although it had belonged to her mother's old aunt, left to Millie in the legacy that bought the *Sandpiper*.

She couldn't flaunt an 'engagement' ring, that would have caused too much comment, but this was nearly as good and she said, 'There's one good reason I shouldn't be here, but so long as you remember we have a deal.'

'Getting to know each other at arm's length,' he said solemnly.

That was exactly what it was. The less he knew about her the better, but she was out for any scrap of information, about him and anybody connected with him, that might help Jack. She had to stay at arm's length to keep her wits about her but it sounded ridiculous, and she laughed a little then said, 'Right.'

'I missed you,' he said.

She hadn't thought she was missing him. She had believed that, given a little more practice and a little more time, she could have stopped thinking about him at all. But the moment she saw him again he had stormed back into her life, and now he was sitting beside her, long and strong and dynamic, she knew that in a way she had missed him. She was more alive and alert when he was around, probably because she had to be.

Right at the beginning Jack had said, 'He's got a mind like a steel trap. One wrong word, one look, could give the game away.' One name certainly would.

If she had said, 'By the way, I'm Jack Perry's sister, and that's the only reason I'm here,' the dark face would darken until he did look like De Flores of *The Changeling*, and although he wouldn't stab her to the heart he would probably destroy her in a less dramatic way, but now he was telling her he had missed her and she said, 'Then you weren't very busy.'

They had stopped at traffic lights and he put a hand on her arm. 'I was, but there was still time to miss you.' He must have felt her jerk back but he made no mention of it taking the wheel again, and it had only been a light touch. 'So what's been happening with you?' he asked and she launched into an account of her last four days.

It had all been humdrum routine but she made him chuckle over some of it. Like Al's misgivings. 'He handed over your key but he wasn't happy about why I went back to the boat with you that night. He thought we were up to no good and I

suppose I should have explained it was because I
thought I was going to be sick after a double cream
meringue on top of a Players production.'

'Good old Al. Although some protection
he'd have been.'

'I don't know. He'd have put a damper on romance. He might have been out for the count but
he was in the only bed.'

'So he was,' and she went gaily on,

'The floor wouldn't have been too healthy and
I've never tried the sofa full-length, but I've sat on
it many a time and it's hard to dodge the broken
springs. That's a genuine relic you've got there. Oh,
and talking of the Players, I had a phone call from
Maud on Saturday; they have these little musical
evenings,' she drawled a mimicry of Maud. 'And
she'd love me to take you along.'

'What did you say?'

'I said I'd tell you.'

'Tell her I'm tone-deaf.'

'Are you?'

'No. Do you go to many of these affairs?'

'I've never been asked before. They're very ex-
clusive. It did occur to me that it could possibly be
just you they wanted.'

Any fool would know that. Maud was a social
climber, and Millie could have told her she was not
getting her VIP. He didn't need to say, 'No, thanks,'
but when he did she laughed.

'I had a call from David Forrest,' he said, and
all the laughter died in her. 'They want us to go
over there. We must fix an evening.'

'That would be lovely,' she said, and thought,
That would be horrific. She would have to find

some excuse to get out of that invitation, although before then Adam might have become bored with her. Or realised that she was not to be trusted. The only sure thing was that the relationship as it seemed to be now would not last, and she shivered so that he raised an eyebrow and she quipped, 'Grey goose walking over my grave. That's a weird saying, isn't it?'

But he looked as if he was wondering what *had* suddenly chilled her blood and she must not let him connect it with David Forrest. She said, 'Tell me something about the folk I'll be meeting. I don't even know who's getting married, nor who your guests are.' When he still seemed thoughtful she said, 'Most of them will know each other. I'll be the odd one out; give me a few clues.'

'This isn't a working holiday. You won't be there to interview them.'

Oh, yes, she would, but she said, 'Of course not. So, what's the name of the bride?'

He humoured her and she listened, bright-eyed as if she was going to a party and hearing who she would be meeting there. Groom and bride. Andrew Calthorpe, whose estate bordered the gardens of the one-time abbey that was the Schofield home. He was the same age as Adam, they had grown up together, and now he was marrying Hilary from a merchant banking family who designed fashion jewellery. That seemed a suitable match all round, Millie thought wryly. Their relations were probably well pleased about that.

He told her about the folk who would be staying at the abbey and she could have done with taking notes, or her little tape recorder would have been

invaluable. As it was she had to file everything in
her mind. While she smiled and asked cheerful
questions, what she really wanted to know was who
were his business contacts, who had the low-down
on his private life, who might discuss him with a
girl they had never met before?

But she mustn't sound too probing and when he
said, 'That should be enough to be going on with,'
she said,

'Yes, it should. I hope they won't mind an extra
guest, I suppose I could always say "Press".'

'You'd do better as a guest.'

'With you I probably would.' Her slanting glance
was mischievous. 'They're expecting you to take
someone along with you, are they? Who are they
expecting?'

The dossier from Jack named names. A couple
of months ago Adam Schofield had been in the
Bahamas, with the daughter of a movie magnate
who was doing quite nicely in the movie business
herself. Perhaps that affair was still on. Nobody
thought Millie was more than a brief encounter,
but it would have been natural for her to ask, 'Who
was your last lady?'

He laughed, glancing at the ring on her right
hand, 'When you tell me more about him I'll tell
you about the one before.'

'That seems a fair swap,' she said.

They stopped for lunch at a fish and seafood restaurant, where Millie realised how hungry she was.
She knew what she had to do during the next few
days, but she could do no more about that right
now and the sensible way to behave was to be seen
to be enjoying herself.

It wasn't too hard. Adam Schofield might be the enemy but he was still fantastic company, and she relaxed and looked at the menu and said, 'I'm starving.'

They started with moules marinière, then Dover sole for Adam and for Millie huge Dublin Bay prawns in garlic butter and a bowl of tangy mayonnaise dip. With crispy salads and fresh vegetables it was a good meal and the lemon tart she chose with her coffee had feather-light pastry.

By then she had slipped into her role so well that she was almost believing she knew nothing sinister about him. That they had met last week, and the physical attraction was strong enough to make her cautious, but she was talking to him as easily as she would have talked to any stunning man who was attracted to her.

She asked about the *Sentinel*, and he said that it was hardly a trail blazer but it did have a solid local readership and he saw no need for change. She asked, 'Why did you buy it?' and he grinned and said it was going cheap.

'How's the novel going?' he asked and a flake of pastry lodged in her throat, making her cough. She had nearly said, What novel?

That first night when he'd enquired if she got bored working on the *Sentinel* she had said her spare time writing was 'steamy sexy stuff'. The scandals she dug up for Jack were usually steamy and sexy, although she had pretended she was talking about a novel.

Now she said, 'I haven't done much this week.'

'May I read it?'

'Nobody reads it. It's private so far.'

'Autobiographical?'

'Not really.'

'You have a vivid imagination?'

'Aren't I lucky?'

He looked at her, smiling, 'A lover and a wild imagination and you're not talking about either. You're a very secretive lady.'

She smiled back. 'Oh, I'm a regular Mona Lisa.' She forked up the last crumbs of her tart, and told him, 'You should have tried this. You can always get cheese but you don't come across a pudding like this every day.' For a moment she had been skating on thin ice but she was surprised how quickly she was cheerful and confident again.

They came to the abbey as night was beginning to fall. Just as she had reached the hotel where Adam was staying in the gloaming and thought that had an eerie look about it. But Alderton Towers was phoney Gothic, while Radstone Abbey was the real thing. It had been the Schofields' home for nearly two hundred years. Inside must have changed out of all recognition but the building ahead of them, with its towers and battlements and tall slit-like windows, looked untouched by time.

In the twilight the light that streamed through windows could have been the flickering of many tapers, and Millie almost expected to hear sonorous voices chanting a litany.

She sat in her seat in the car, silent and awe-struck, until Adam came round and opened her door, and then she said, '*How* long is it since the monks left?'

He had told her that after Henry VIII and the Reformation this was an abbey in name only but now he said, with mock solemnity, 'Some say they never did.'

'You've got ghosts, of course?'

'None I've come across myself, but they're supposed to walk where the cloisters used to be.'

'Well, they would, wouldn't they?' She scrambled out of the car, staring in wonder. 'What a place to grow up in.' She meant what a marvellously exciting place, but he said,

'Now you see why I like boats and lighthouses,' and she laughed.

'Where there's nothing to spook you but Al.'

'And that's a ghost you could dump in the river.'

'No, you couldn't. Not my lovely old Al.'

The monks had never had it like this. Through the massive wooden doors into the warmth and light everything was splendidly luxurious, the home of a very rich man. Jack had not got a fraction of Adam Schofield's resources and although Millie smiled, because the woman and the man coming towards her were smiling, she was scared for her brother. And for herself, sent in here as his spy.

The man and the woman were staff. Others had to be guests and they all seemed to be talking at once, hailing Adam and eyeing Millie.

Adam said, 'Be right with you,' and guided Millie towards the wide staircase that curved up to the gallery. 'You'd like to freshen up?' he said.

'Yes, I would.'

The journey had been longish. She was rumpled and her travelling top-coat was serviceable rather than stylish. She wanted to redo her face, fix her hair, get out of this bulky coat into a flattering dress. Because she knew that the women staying here were going to be class acts, every one.

Not that Millie was competing. They had nothing she wanted, and that included Adam Schofield. But when she went down to join them she was determined to be looking her best.

The man who had met them in the hall was carrying her case and after rounding a couple of corners in the panelled corridor and passing another staircase Adam opened a door and said, 'Here you are. Half an hour?'

'I'll be ready.' She would have no time to waste but she could do it, although this was a room she would have enjoyed lingering in. A fire burned in the grey-stone fireplace, a cream-covered bed was set against a cream silk-lined wall, and there were sofas, chairs, a writing desk, exquisite water-colours of flowers in thin oval frames.

A girl came through a door leading into a bathroom, said, 'Good evening, madam, may I unpack for you?' and when Millie said that was all right she was left alone.

She did her own unpacking, hanging clothes in a rosewood cupboard that turned out to be the wardrobe, and laying a pale mint and pink polka-dotted dress for this evening on the bed. She promised herself a long spell in the gorgeous bathroom later, but now she wasted no time and she was ready with just five minutes to spare.

Then she went to the window for the first time.

Below her were lawns, stretching to what was probably the cliff's edge because she could hear the sea when she opened the latticed window a little. Heavy clouds floated across the moon but there was light enough to sense the vastness of this building and the loneliness of the sea out there.

She loved the sea, like the river only bigger and wilder, and one day she might get the boat that would sail to fabulous places over fathomless oceans.

At the tap on the door she left the window, gave herself a fleeting glance in the mirror of a Victorian dressing-table—she was no model girl but she wasn't bad—and went to where Adam was waiting.

He was freshly shaved and well groomed, and the understated elegance of his grey suit, grey shirt and dark grey tie was belied by the impact of his striking good looks and the strong planes of his face and wide mouth. The charm was there but surely nobody could miss the toughness.

Millie made herself smile—she was doing such a lot of that—and indicated her dress and herself asking, 'All right?'

'Absolutely,' he said and when he almost touched her she swayed back and pretended to joke,

'That's near enough.'

'No,' he said, 'not nearly near enough,' but he was smiling and it was a joke, although she must stop flushing. From now on she would be sensible. She said, 'It is the sea, isn't it, that I can see through my windows? The lawns are to the cliff's edge?'

'Yes, that's where the cloisters were. There are still a few stones left.'

'Where the grey ghosts walk?'

'These ghosts wore brown; they were Franciscans.'

'But you've never seen one?'

'No. Perhaps I lack your imagination.' He smiled down at her. 'If you strike lucky, call me.'

She said lightly, 'I promise, but I'm not psychic.'

They were walking along the corridor that ended on the gallery and when he took her hand this time she let her fingers lie loosely in his. 'So apart from your steamy sexy novel,' he said, 'you don't go in for fantasies?' and she gave a small shake of the head. 'Just for secrets,' he said.

At the top of the great staircase they were facing each other. He had looked at her this way before, in his suite that first night when he had said he doubted if she was what she seemed. He was remembering too, and that she had said, 'So what am I?' because now he said softly, 'I will find out, Millie.'

She clenched her jaw so that it looked as if she was smiling still and said, 'That is the idea, getting to know each other.'

She wanted to go home. No, not home, except to get Flower and then to run all the way to the *Sandpiper*. She thought, I cannot be doing this. They're not going to tell me anything and if they do I won't know what Jack can use and what he can't. And well before Friday Adam is going to find out what I'm about, or seduce me, or both, and either way I shall be torn apart.

She took a blind step away from him, stumbling at the top of the stairs, and he grabbed her and shook her, slightly so that it was hardly a shake although his voice shook, 'For God's sake, Millie, if you're accident prone you must be used to this— first you nearly smash into a car and then you

almost throw yourself down the stairs—but I am
not used to it and you are giving me heart failure.'

'Sorry,' she stammered, 'I'm not usually clumsy;
anyhow, why should you care?'

'Because I care about you. You matter to me.'
He was not smiling. He held her still, looking down
at her, and her near-fall must have shaken her because her heart was hammering madly. There were
people down in the hall but she could only hear and
see him.

'Chemistry I've come across before,' he said, 'but
this is different, and how can I work out why it's
different if I'm so scared of losing you it poleaxes
me?'

This was just talk, he couldn't mean this, but
there was something in his eyes that made the breath
catch in her throat and she heard herself say
breathlessly, 'It is just chemistry. I don't have your
experience but I can tell you that. And I'll tell you
something else, it had damn well better be.'

The watchers downstairs had seen her lurch at
the top of the staircase, seen Adam steady her and
speak to her. Their voices had been too quiet to be
overheard, but the guests saw them begin to laugh,
both of them, and come down the stairs smiling.

As Adam introduced her she ticked them off in
her mind: the MP, the TV producer, the property
developer, the lawyer, the charity organiser. They
were not all beautiful people but they looked successful and they gave Millie the impression that they
could have formed a cosy little club.

If they hadn't known each other before, they had
found each other congenial company, and they all
knew Adam Schofield and they were all interested,

particularly the women, in the woman he had brought home with him.

Millie was an easy adapter, and her time as a newspaper reporter had developed her flair as a good listener. Talk flowed around her and her fellow guests soon accepted the pretty girl with the green-flecked eyes, who sparkled even when she was silent, and laughed at the jokes.

Over dinner she was seated on the right of Adam, who headed the table, and on her left was the man in horn-rimmed spectacles, from the cutting in the dossier, next to his wife. If anyone knew about Adam Schofield Peter Barkin should. He had worked for Schofield Enterprises ever since they both left university in the same year, and Millie wondered if she might get a chance for a one-to-one talk later.

Barkin headed the communications section now and as a dinner guest he was witty and chatty, but he had sharp eyes behind the spectacles and she couldn't imagine him being indiscreet, telling her anything Jack didn't know.

Adam told them he had taken over a narrowboat, and then Barkin told them about the narrowboat Adam had had on the Oxford canal, and how it had listed and sunk with hardly any warning the first time Adam's grandfather had been persuaded to set foot on it.

There was an oil painting of the haughty hawk-faced old gentleman on the dining-room wall. He looked as though nothing would make him move fast and Millie asked, like an idiot, 'Did he get ashore?'

Adam said, 'He certainly did.'

'There were only the three of us and he was first off without turning a hair,' said Peter. 'Then he stood on the bank and watched it sinking. He enjoyed that.' The men grinned at each other, sharing a hilarious memory; and most of the conversation was entertaining.

Some of the news swapping about mutual acquaintances was malicious, maybe scandalous, but Adam didn't join in the malice and she didn't know how to link it up with him. Sometimes they talked about their work. But even when politics came up the arguments were mild, and always it seemed simply a pleasant dinner party where guests were enjoying themselves in a civilised fashion.

Although when it was realised how late it was and the party broke up, everyone heading for their rooms but Adam, Peter Barkin and the property developer, Millie wished she could have been a fly on the wall. Those three might discuss things that Jack might like to hear about.

She had drunk very little wine but it had been a long day and she had to be tired; only in the morning she might not be able to recall half of it so she kicked off her shoes and lay on the bed in the darkness, talking into her hand-recorder.

She gave the names first: who they were, what they did, like the cast of a play. And then, as near as she could, she dictated their words. With eyes closed and concentrating fiercely she was managing to relive that scene downstairs and repeat most of the table talk.

She finished 'Adam and Peter Barkin and Frank Poole went into what seemed to be a study, but I could hardly follow them in there so that's all.'

Then she clicked off and lay for a little while listening to the sound of the sea, the window was still ajar, until the mind she had been forcing into overdrive slowed down, and the tension began to leave her.

Then at last, she padded across the carpet to the window, cooling her hot forehead against the stone of the window frame. There was still some light from the house, and moonlight came and went, and when she looked down she saw the figure where the cloisters used to be.

It was Adam, walking alone. She knew that at once, and at the same time she felt a tremendous urge to go down and join him. The fire was down to embers in the grate but the room was warm and suddenly it seemed that a breath of cool sea air would be a life saver. She had been cooped up in a car all day, and sitting round a table all evening; now she wanted to stretch her legs and her lungs and go out on to the cliff top.

She pulled on boots and buttoned up her top coat, and hurried down the stairs at the end of the corridor. It was no surprise that the door at the bottom led to the back of the house—obviously it would—and she stepped out on to flagstones and then on to lawns.

Adam was still there. A cloud drifted across the moon but she could see him clearly, and he saw her and came to meet her. When he reached her he said, 'I hoped you'd come,' and it was as though he had known that she would. As though he had called her.

CHAPTER FIVE

WHEN Millie reached Adam he put an arm around
her shoulders and it seemed the most natural thing
in the world. Tomorrow her antagonism could flare
as fiercely as ever but out here in the shifting
moonlight, with the sea crashing on the rocks below
and the ancient abbey looming above them, a
strange magic was in the air.

They walked the cloisters. Under the grass she
could feel the odd stone that was all that remained
of the paved ways, surrounded by arches, along
which the hooded monks in their brown habits had
walked on sandalled feet.

Adam told her the cloisters had gone with the
sacking of the abbey. Most of the stones that
remained had been used in repairs to the rest of the
building when it was turned into a fortified manor
house for one of the king's cronies. Later the whole
place was almost a ruin until an ancestor of Adam's
had rebuilt it two hundred years ago.

'And it's been like this ever since?'

'Not quite.' On the cliff's edge they were turning
to look back. 'My grandfather was a landowner;
he thought the money would come in for ever. My
father died in a plane crash...' She knew that—
both his father and his mother before Adam
reached his teens. 'He'd been going through resources at a rate of knots. When my grandfather
died we were heading for bankruptcy.'

The dossier hadn't said that, nor had Jack. Perhaps that wasn't generally known, but now Schofield Enterprises were riding high. She asked, 'What did you do?'

'Sold off here and there and got to work.' He sounded as if it had been easy but of course it hadn't. 'I was lucky,' he said. 'I've usually been lucky.'

The wind was blowing her hair across her face. He held it back with gentle fingers. 'Never luckier than when I met you,' he said, and she hoped the night was dark enough to hide the flame of colour that sprang up in her cheeks.

There was a handrail here, a path leading down and beach below, and she asked, 'Can we go down?' because his cool fingers must feel the heat in her face, and she had to turn her head away.

'Do you want to go down?'

'Please,' she said.

The path was steep, but safe enough if you held the iron handrail and watched your step. Adam went just ahead of her and at the bottom was shifting shingle, pebbles and rocks. High tide mark gleamed in the moonlight, the tide had turned now and they walked to where the foam was still breaking at their feet.

She looked for the lighthouse and he pointed. 'It's hard to see in this light but it's on the rocks to the right out there. You can walk to it at low tide, or use a dinghy, of course.'

'Will you take me there some time?'

'Of course.'

Even after the wedding his house might still be full of guests but surely they would find some time

to be alone together, and tonight she was beginning
to wonder if she could talk to him. He was talking
to her as though he trusted her and knew she would
understand. She did understand. Saving the abbey,
buying the lighthouse, were things she would have
wanted desperately to do herself if she had been in
his position. She might even manage to tell him
about Jack and ask him to go easy, although
nobody must know that Jack was her brother. It
was a terrible tangle but there must be some way
that would mean she no longer had to act the spy.

'What are you thinking about?' She had been
looking thoughtful and now she said, quickly,

'Just how lovely it all is. I was terribly impressed
by your other guests.'

He contradicted her flatly, 'No, you weren't.'

'I *was*, I liked them.'

'I didn't say you didn't like them. So do I, but
you weren't terrifically impressed by anybody and
why should you be? Although I noticed you didn't
do much talking yourself.'

She should have expected him to notice, he didn't
miss much, and she carried it on as a joke, 'For
someone who usually rattles on, you mean? Oh, I
do listen, you know—it's my job to listen.' She
shouldn't have put it that way but he laughed and
she changed the subject, breathing the wet salty air
and telling him one of her own small dreams.

'I love the sea. One day I'll have a bigger boat
than the *Sandpiper* and sail away to the Greek
islands.'

'I do have a bigger boat. Will you sail with me?'

She was as delighted as if it was going to happen, and it might, and if it did it would be a fantastic adventure. She said, 'I'd be a good deck-hand.'

'Just what I had in mind for you.' He grinned wickedly and she laughed, swaying a little from the breeze and the wet sand beneath her feet, and he seemed as strong and steady as the rocks. As if she could have turned to him and leaned on him through anything.

The sea was choppy and clouds scudded across the dark sky and she wondered, 'What will the weather be like for the wedding?'

'Stormy.'

'Looks like it. I brought a hat.' She had bought a hat, a navy blue straw. Nothing flashy, she wasn't a real guest at this wedding. The spray in the air had settled like a mist on her skin and on her hair. She pushed her fingers through her hair now. 'I'll either have to wash my hair tonight or wear my hat pulled well down.'

'So you think we should turn back?'

'I think I should.'

'I insist on seeing you home.'

'You always did.' So he had. Except when she drove her own car back from Alderton Towers, shaken out of her wits by that first kiss. He hadn't kissed her since. He had hardly touched her since but the attraction was stronger than ever and he was right, it wasn't just chemistry.

As they crossed the lawns she said, 'The Franciscans were the Order of St Francis, weren't they? And he was the saint who loved animals so perhaps I should have brought Flower.'

Adam smiled. 'Does he know he's a dog? He doesn't think he's your big brother?'

And Millie had to draw in a long breath before she could say lightly, 'Sometimes, maybe.'

There was movement in the house, lights were still on, but they passed nobody climbing the stairs or walking along the corridor. They might have passed Adam's room; she didn't know which that was and she didn't ask. She hoped he wouldn't want to share hers, she wasn't quite ready for that. But at her door he said, 'Goodnight.'

'Goodnight,' she said gratefully. She lifted her face for his kiss and it warmed her as though she had been held in his arms for hours. He touched the ring on her right hand and said,

'Don't sleep in that, I don't want you dreaming of him.'

She almost said, 'I made him up,' but perhaps it wasn't yet the time for that either. So she said, 'I never do sleep in it,' and when she got into her room the first thing she did was take off the ring. The next was to put her tape recorder into her case which locked, and then she started to undress.

She washed her hair under the shower and rubbed it dry with a towel, kneeling in front of the dying fire. Her hair was thick and well cut. She should be able to coax it so that it looked all right tomorrow. Tomorrow, she was beginning to hope, everything would be all right.

She woke to find a girl with a tea-tray standing by her bed and could hardly believe how deeply and dreamlessly she had slept. She ran her own bath and went to the window wrapped in a towel to check on the weather. Stormy was about right. The clouds seemed darker than ever, threatening a deluge of rain although it was not raining yet.

She could see the outline of the lighthouse now, rising on a little rocky island below a sheer cliff face. Adam had said he would take her out there and that might be the place and time to tell him about Jack. Last night she had been sure she could make him understand, although she knew how bitter and deep-rooted the enmity was between the two men. But she was less confident in the cold light of day.

If she did get the chance and there seemed to be any hope at all she would take it, but she was no longer certain the opportunity would arise. Nor how she would put her case if it did.

They were going down to breakfast dressed for the wedding. Millie's suit would have been suitable for any smart casual affair, even for the well dressed office. It was a straight navy skirt and a short fuchsia jacket trimmed with navy braid, worn with navy pumps, a white blouse and a navy fine straw hat. She looked young and fresh and pretty but the other women all looked sensational. Peter Barkin's wife, Monique, in green and gold, could have stepped straight off a couture show catwalk.

The men were in more or less matching grey or black morning suits, although when Adam came out of the office there was nobody who looked like him. It wasn't clothing, it was what he was, the force of him that dominated without a word being spoken.

As he walked towards Millie she thought, I could be so proud of you; and when he reached her he looked at her as if he was proud of her, and the other women *were* stunning but Millie was beginning to feel rather good herself.

It drizzled on the way to church. Millie drove there with Adam, Peter and Monique, and Monique chattered with a charming French accent about all manner of things, from their own son and Adam's godson, who was four years old and staying with Peter's parents while they were here, to a cottage in Provence they were considering buying.

Millie sat back in the comfortable seat and watched the slow seeping rain, and listened to Monique without waiting for anything she could pass on to Jack. She was taking today as it came. It was a holiday and she was enjoying herself and maybe a little miracle would happen.

The church had been built for a village congregation, which meant it was full, and a fair-sized crowd of onlookers had gathered on the pavements, because everyone in these parts knew the Calthorpes and most of them were used to seeing Hilary Fleming around.

Inside the church was a bower of greenery. They were guided to their seats and walking down the aisle Millie was getting more attention than Monique. It was attention she could have done without as necks craned and whispers hissed, 'Who's that with Adam Schofield?' 'No idea, never seen her before.' 'Not much, compared with some he's had, is she?'

And she was not imagining it, she could hear them even though the organ was booming away.

The groom, tall, fair and good-looking, was sitting beside the best man, who had to be his

brother or a first cousin. They were more alike than
Millie and her brother, and she glanced quickly at
Adam, as though he might be reading her thoughts.

'Sorry I let you in for this,' he said, 'but I wanted
you to come down here.'

'I wanted to come too,' she said, and the organ
music changed to the bridal march, and everyone
including Millie turned to see the bride on her
father's arm, with half a dozen small pages and
bridesmaids bobbing along behind.

Millie thought she was beautiful. She *was*
beautiful, in a long white glittering dress, hood,
sleeves and skirt, edged in swansdown so that she
looked like a fairytale snow princess.

Millie had been to lots of weddings, some were
friends, some were local socialites whose weddings
she was reporting for the *Sentinel*, but she had never
felt like this before. As she watched these two, who
were strangers to her, taking their vows... love,
honour and cherish... sickness and in health... till
death us do part... her throat became tight and
aching.

She thought, I hope they will be happy, I hope
they never hurt each other. And she was agonisingly
aware of Adam beside her and of the gulf between
them. Any closeness was a myth while she was
cheating all the way. She would have to tell him,
and then he might never want to see her again, and
she bit on her underlip, holding down a gulp that
was almost a sob.

He took her hand and she looked up at him and
it took a mighty effort to raise a ghost of a smile.
'I'm always a fool at weddings,' she whispered.
He'd think she was thinking about that 'secret' lover

of hers, and in a way she was because that lie was part of the deception.

He could have no idea what was really troubling her but he said quietly, 'It's going to be all right,' and she said,

'Promises, promises,' because she had to say something and because if he could promise that it would be her little miracle.

The reception was held in the whole ground floor of a big old farmhouse, spilling into a large marquee, and everybody who couldn't get into the little church seemed to have turned up for the speeches and the cake-cutting and the buffet and the never-ending trays of champagne that were being carried around.

She lost Adam. He was grabbed time and again wherever he turned, and after a couple of glasses of champagne Millie found it easier to make her own way around. When Adam looked for her and he did, she signalled back that she was fine, and there were plenty of people willing to talk to her. They wanted to know who she was and where she had come from, and then they usually talked about Adam.

The woman charity organiser, who was among the guests at the abbey, told her that Adam gave a lot to charity, always insisting the gifts were anonymous. Jack would have put that down to tax fiddles, but it might not be and she didn't think she would mention it. She was hearing nothing that would interest Jack. As Adam's friend it was unlikely she would but he did seem to be popular down here.

'You're the gel with Adam Schofield.' Millie had heard that a few times. This was from a horse-faced woman, wearing a suit in magenta check that looked rather like a horse blanket. When Millie admitted that she was, she got a head-to-foot inspection, and a brief, 'Hmm,' after which the lady in magenta strode away.

Then Millie heard Peter chuckle and realised he was watching, and grinned at him. 'Well, she didn't seem to like the look of me.'

'You look too good,' he said. 'She had designs on Adam for her daughter.'

She won't be the only one, thought Millie, and she asked gaily, 'Did he have designs on her daughter?'

'No,' said Peter, and they both looked across to where someone else had managed to draw Adam into their group. 'But he is a star attraction.'

'I had noticed that.'

'So why aren't you over there?'

She laughed, 'It must be the reporter in me: keep moving and listening.' She was trying to joke but that had a bitter undertone and she didn't want to talk about herself. She said lightly, 'Are you a fan?'

'Always was, always will be.' His voice was as light as hers but he meant that.

'You must know him as well as anybody.'

'I think so.' And she had to ask,

'How deep is the charm? Skin deep?'

'Not even that.' Light from a great chandelier up there in the apex of the marquee glittered on his spectacles, but when he turned his head slightly his eyes seemed so shrewd and sharp that she wondered if he needed glasses at all. 'Scratch him and they'd find out,' he said.

He was probably warning her. She raised her eyebrows. 'So he's got enemies as well as friends?' She knew it. Even if she hadn't she would have presumed that anyone making his way to the top as Adam had done would have made enemies.

'He's a very private man,' said Peter. 'Most of them haven't the remotest idea what he's like.'

'I guess not.' He *was* warning her. He was feeling sorry for her, and for the life of her she couldn't resist taking advantage of that.

She put on her wide-eyed little-girl face and the voice to match. 'I didn't know much about him until your firm bought up the paper I work for. There were snippets in the Press, I suppose, but I don't read the business pages much. I do remember two or three years back there was some sort of scandal. What was her name—Sharon somebody?'

Nearly everyone in here seemed to be talking at once and at the top of their voices. The noise was deafening but a cold little silence touched Millie as Peter Barkin looked steadily at her. Then he said, 'Have you discussed this with Adam?'

He knew she had been trying to pump him and he was having none of it. She shook her head. 'No, I've only just thought of it.' That was wildly unlikely and he asked,

'Shall I get you some food?' as if the champagne might have gone to her head and perhaps it had.

'No, thank you,' she said.

He looked for his wife but before he moved away he said, 'Don't try to dig too deep,' as if she was going to make a fool of herself and get hurt in the process. And he would have been staggered to know how right he was on both counts.

After that she went back to the buffet and filled a small plate with bite-sized sandwiches. She ate slowly, and then she was going to find Adam and stay with him, because although she was not the least jealous she was suddenly thoroughly bored with everyone else.

Adam found her when she had just one sandwich left, and at the touch of his hand on her shoulder and the sound of his voice she felt her smile widen until she must be grinning like the Cheshire cat. 'I was just coming to find you,' she told him.

He took her last sandwich and said, 'Not a moment too soon. How do you feel about dancing the night away?'

'What?'

'That's the idea. Any time now we're getting a group who could be fiddling till dawn.'

She wouldn't mind, she had danced all night before now, but Adam was checking his watch and telling her, 'It will be low tide in half an hour; how about going out to the lighthouse?'

'I must be getting old, I couldn't possibly dance till dawn,' she said solemnly with sparkling eyes. 'But will they let you get away?'

'Can you see anyone here who could stop us?' They were in the crowded marquee but she thought, I've never seen anybody anywhere who could stop you; and somehow they were out of a door, and going fast for the car park, at a rate that left her breathless.

Rain was still falling, the skies were still dark, but she was as elated as if the sun had burst

through. She could have hugged herself with glee.
In the car she took off her hat and let her head fall
back.

'Do you want music?' he asked.

'No, do you mind?'

'I don't mind at all.'

She had been under inspection every minute in
there. Most of the time somebody had been talking
to her, or at her. Now there was only the powerful
purr of the engine, and the slight movements of the
man at the wheel beside her like a rhythm, a beat
in her blood. She was in tune with him and the
music was magical.

They reached the abbey too soon. She wanted to
see inside the lighthouse but that had been a lovely
ride. Garages, which had once been carriage and
coach-houses, were at the side of the house, and as
he drew up Adam enquired, 'Do you want to
change?'

Neither was dressed for scrambling over rocks,
but now she was here Millie was suddenly scared
that if they wasted time something would stop them
or somebody else would join them. She asked, 'Can
we walk out now?'

'Yes.'

'I'm fine.' Her pumps had flat heels, her suit
could be cleaned and pressed. 'How about you?'

'Wait here,' he said. 'I'll get some oilskins.'

'Hurry,' she said. She stood under an
overhanging roof, hoping there were no urgent
messages waiting for him so that he would come
back and say, 'Sorry, we can't make it right now,
we can always take a boat out some time.'

But she wanted to go now, over the sands or under the cliffs, whichever way it was; and then when the tide turned they would be there for a while, alone together away from the rest of his guests.

They wouldn't all be dancing the night away. Some of them might be returning to the abbey as soon as they realised that Adam had left. Millie had never been possessive about any man before, but Adam drew the crowds and Millie had had enough of crowds for a while.

He came back wearing a long yellow oilskin and carrying another, smaller and shorter although it almost reached Millie's ankles, and with the hood pulled up she could only see straight ahead like a blinkered horse. So she shoved back the hood and with the coat fastened up to the neck she was well covered.

But it flapped about her in the wind crossing the cloisters on the cliff top, and going down the cliff path it wrapped around her legs so that more than once Adam had to steady her.

She wouldn't have a scrap of make-up left by the time they reached the lighthouse. She hadn't been prepared for this but it was exhilarating, with the lighthouse to make for and the rocks shining with weeds like rippling green satin.

They went beneath overhanging cliffs, between rock pools and little gulleys where the sea still eddied, and the lighthouse loomed higher as they got closer. A tall straight tower, four storeys high, with a sea wall built around it and steps hacked in the rocks and leading up to a porch.

She needed the handrail, it had been tough getting here, and as Adam opened the door she leaned against the porch and tipped wet shale out of her shoes. When he picked her up she laughed as they went through the doorway. 'Now I get a lift! Where were you when I was climbing rocks?'

'You were managing over the rocks. This is "welcome aboard".'

'Carrying a woman over the threshold? Haven't you got the wrong tradition?'

'Have I?' He put her down and grinned. 'Well, it seemed a good idea at the time.'

She was going to say something jokey but when she looked round she gasped. He had bought the lighthouse over ten years ago, when it ceased to operate with keepers and new automatic lighthouses took over along the coast. She had expected it to have been converted into a luxurious pad. No expense need have been spared, but he couldn't have changed it at all.

The floor was flagstoned with a couple of large rugs worn down to the nap, and a big iron stove looked as if it had been fitted in when the lighthouse was built. A brass-rimmed clock and framed maps and charts hung on the curved walls, which were painted deep cream and could have done with a freshener.

She stared around her. 'You haven't changed a thing.'

'Not much down here. The equipment was moved out before I got it.'

Why should he have changed anything? If he wanted opulence there was the abbey. This was special, unique. As she fumbled with the fasteners of her coat she looked at the charts, peering because the narrow windows were inset in thick walls so that the natural light was not too good in here.

Night would be falling before long but there were lamps. Adam was lighting an oil-lamp on a big scrubbed-top table, and two Davy lamps hung from the beams. She heard the crackle of wood and turned to see flames leaping in the stove with the iron doors opened. It was not all that different from the stove in the narrowboat. He probably wouldn't change that either, and she smiled, 'You can leave things alone, can't you? That gives me hope for the *Sentinel.*'

'But I didn't buy the *Sentinel* as a bolt-hole.'

'Is that what the narrowboat is?'

'No, the narrowboat's because I like boats. *This* is a bolt-hole.'

He was smiling too and she said, 'But they can still get at you here.'

'Not if they know what's good for them. Nobody comes out here after me.'

'So when is the brasswork polished and the fire laid?'

'When I'm not here.'

'You've got it made.' She unpopped the final stud and stepped out of the oilskin. His was hanging on a hook beside the door and he took hers and looped it alongside. When she asked, 'Was it always a bolt-hole?' he seemed to hesitate before he told her,

'Always. I was coming out here as long as I can remember. Over the rocks or on the boat with the provisions, bringing or taking off the keepers. My grandfather was a splendid old chap, but he wasn't on the same planet as these men.'

'What happened to them?'

'They were all coming up to retirement age. There were four of them. Two are still alive.'

'You keep in touch?'

'Oh, yes, I keep in touch.'

Jack didn't know what the lighthouse meant to Adam. In the dossier it would be included in 'property around the abbey' owned by Schofield. Millie was learning things and there was only one thing she could tell Adam about herself that was not common knowledge. But not yet. She needed more time to find the courage and the words.

'Shall I show you around?' he said.

'Please.'

Old log books were in the cupboards and she would enjoy leafing through them. She turned a few pages carefully. Two of the old lighthouse keepers were still around and she would like to talk to them and learn how it was when Adam was very young. Not for Jack. For herself.

Steps going up curved round the wall and up there two bunks followed the same curve. The bottom bunk had a duvet and she asked, 'You sleep out here?'

'Sometimes.'

The bunks were narrow and there was only one duvet. 'But you don't expect company?'

'No.' He had company now. But a talking companion, not a sleeping one. She was almost sure that was understood.

Darkness was closing in and he carried a lamp. The upper storeys were empty, but the windows were still intact and the top of the tower provided a fantastic look-out.

When he turned down the lamp there seemed to be no ships out there, nothing showing a light. There was a moon when the clouds weren't covering it. You could watch all the stars on a clear night. And the storms when they came. She said, 'You'd feel you were in the eye of a storm up here.'

'Storms can be spectacular. Down below green water can rise higher than the windows. The walls can shake.'

She could imagine. Looking out from this high tower, across the sea and skies where nothing living seemed to move, was awesome, and she smiled a little at her fantasy, 'We could be the only people in the world.'

'"What if this present were the world's last night?"' he quoted.

'What?'

'John Donne.'

She quoted too, ' "Come live with me and be my love. And we will some new pleasures prove".'

'That's the one.'

The poet had lived years before Adam's ancestors rebuilt the abbey but his words were timeless. She said, 'If it were the world's last night——' and paused, unsaid words trembling on her parted lips... There is no place I would rather be and no one I would rather be with... She could almost believe she had said that aloud, it rang so clearly in her mind; and it scared her because it was true.

She shivered, wrapping her own arms around herself, and Adam said, 'It's cold up here.' He turned the wick of the lamp up again, so that all the brightness was around them and the stairway down was well lit.

The fire and the oil lamps had already warmed up the room. Now it looked cosy, scruffy and lived in. She went to the fire, realising how damp her feet were and taking off her shoes. That was how this had started, with her hopping barefoot in front of an old iron stove. Adam was opening a cupboard and she said, 'I must wear gumboots more often.'

'That would be a shame. You've got legs that shouldn't be hidden.'

It hadn't started in the narrowboat, of course. It had started when she'd learned that Jack was her brother and Adam was her enemy. But the first time she had seen Adam was in the *Sentinel* office, and the first time she'd talked with him was that night on the narrowboat.

She wished that had been the real beginning, with no bitter background, because from then on her life had been filled with excitement and shared laughter, and a sensuous awakening that was dangerous but thrilling, like being in a canoe without a paddle rushing on to the rapids.

She laughed at the compliment. 'Thank you— they're not bad are they, my legs?'

'Almost irresistible. That's why you sat in that chair on the narrowboat with your feet tucked well under.'

She sat on a flock-covered couch now, 'I didn't think I looked irresistible so much as a bit of a prat. By the way, have you ever sat in that wooden armchair?'

'No.'

'Well, when you do, don't lean to the left because it can tip over. Al didn't tell you?'

'No.'

'I suppose he's stopped noticing.'

'Anything else you should warn me against?'

Only myself! 'You can take care of yourself,' she said.

'Not when chairs give way under me.'

'But you can pick yourself up.'

'Oh, yes,' he said, 'I can always do that.' He had taken down a bottle of red wine and was pouring it into two glasses. There were tins and packages on the shelves of the cupboard. 'Try this,' he said.

He sat down beside her and the suspension was better in this couch than in Al's sofa; this was quite firm and springy. Adam looked very distinguished in black morning suit and white shirt. The hike over here hardly seemed to have roughed him up at all; even his hair had fallen back into well groomed order.

A man of impeccable taste, which extended to his wine selection, because she knew without asking that this was an excellent vintage. Not that it would have been her choice. It was too rich for her palate, too strong. Like him, she thought, too strong and too rich, and she was wondering if she could make a joke of that, because she had grimaced instinctively at the first swallow, when he said, 'Take it slowly, you could get to like it.'

She wasn't taking him slowly. In a matter of hours she had known she was madly attracted to him. But they were talking about the wine and she teased, 'That might not be a good idea; where would I get my next bottle?'

'If it is the world's last night what's here should be enough for both of us.'

'But it isn't. Is it?'

'I hope not.'

'It just—feels like that.' They were joking but not smiling. Perhaps not joking. She was so conscious of him that nothing outside these walls seemed real. He must have taken the glass out of her hand and put down his own because he held her hand in both of his and she felt the touch to her fingertips and along the inside of her arm.

She had never had this kind of physical reaction before and she croaked, 'Chemistry.'

'Chemistry and what?'

'Lord knows.' She started to talk, hearing the desperate brightness in her voice, 'Peter Barkin said that nobody there today really knows you. Except him.'

'He's a good friend.'

'"Don't dig too deep," he said. I think he meant that I might find something that would frighten me to death.'

Adam raised an ironic eyebrow. 'He does know me better than most, but he doesn't know you. You're not going to be frightened to death.'

'No?'

'Because you are tough as old boots.'

Maybe not that tough, but she was tougher than she looked and she drawled, 'Charming!'

'That too,' he said. 'You could sit out there and charm the sailors on to the rocks any time,' and that made her laugh,

'My hair's too short. Sirens had to comb their long green hair. And sing. I don't have much of a voice. It's Maud you need out here.'

'It's not Maud I need, anywhere.'

Peter would tell Adam what she had said. She had better tell him first, and she said, 'I shocked Peter.'

'This gets interesting.'

'I asked him about Sharon Ward.'

'And what did you think he could tell you about her?'

'Nothing,' she said, and shrugged, making nothing of it, wishing she hadn't brought up the name at all.

It had happened a long time ago, when Adam Schofield was making headlines because of a major takeover and this girl had gone to Jack with her story. Adam Schofield had been her lover. There had been a torrid affair during which he had kept her prisoner for several weeks in a house on the Yorkshire moors in the dead of winter.

The girl's kiss-and-tell made red-hot reading and Jack was launching a media deal when she'd backed out and denied the whole thing. Either bought off or scared off, and Schofield had targeted the publicist with a libel action that was settled out of court with Jack paying heavy damages.

'I had no bloody choice,' he'd told Millie. 'Schofield had the clout and he crippled me.' She believed Jack and she was angry for him, but it was a long time ago and right now the present seemed all that mattered, this hour, this night. This man.

She went into his arms and this was where she had to be, safe in the eye of the storm. Because there was a storm. She could hear the wind rising, feel her skin warming and all her pulses beating faster.

He kissed her and this kiss was sweet, a touch of tongues. Then he lifted his head and looked into her eyes and said, 'Millie?' as if he was questioning, and she made no sound but her lips framed yes.

She had a hand on his arm, feeling the hard muscles beneath the sleeve of his jacket. She slipped off her own jacket, and he put a hand on her breast and kissed her again: eyelids, tip of her nose, brushing her lips and reaching the pulse on her throat. Staying there while her head went back and he slowly unbuttoned her shirt and she slid out of that and the straps of her bra.

Her outstretched fingers went round his ribcage, gripping so that his steely strength and the hammer of his heartbeats were becoming part of her, and when he stripped she watched, marvelling, and reached for him greedily.

Then she lay still, and there were cool hands on every inch of her: shoulders, arms, the length of her body, legs, feet. And everywhere the caresses went under her skin so that she could never forget them. And she began to touch him, and taste the salt on him like the sea, and thought, I would know you naked if I were blind.

Then the storm that was rising in her went wild. Higher and higher, fiercer and fiercer, and when it climaxed it came like all the thunder and lightning in the world, bonding her body and soul with the man.

Together in a total embrace, over the rapids or riding the storm, she was in every part of him, and he was touching her heart, deep inside her, and then she was floating down into deep still waters, her limbs getting heavier, heavier, so that she could have slept for ever, rocked in his arms.

But she could feel his breath on her face and when she opened her eyes he was looking down at her, smiling, 'Your eyes are green,' he said.

'Not all the time.' She was drowsy but she blinked her eyes into wakefulness. 'It must be the sea-water. There was a storm, wasn't there? The tower did shake?'

'That it did,' he said. The storm had been of their making but she was slippery with sweat as if she had been in the sea, and she sat up and looked for her clothes.

'Don't,' he said. 'Wait.' He brought down the duvet from the bunkroom above and wrapped it around her. 'I should be making a feast for you,' he said.

She said, 'You did,' and began to smile because she was hungry. Any minute her stomach could start rumbling and she asked, 'What do you have in the cupboard?'

'Iron rations. Nothing that seems to fit the bill. It should be champagne and caviare.'

'We should have brought a selection from the wedding buffet.'

'Too late for that now.'

'I'd settle for beans on toast.'

'No bread, no toast. Beans, yes.'

She reached for her clothes. 'Sorry, but if I'm coming out from under the duvet I need these. And the bathroom.'

'I'll open tins,' he said.

The bathroom was small and chilly. There was running water from a storage tank but it was so cold that she settled for dabbling her hands and face, and when she was dressed she was glad the shaving mirror was small, and so high she had to stand on tiptoe to see herself at all because she must look a wreck. But in the living-room the lamplight was mellow and flattering.

Adam was in black trousers, barefoot and shirtless, with the shadow of a dark beard. There was shaving stuff in the bathroom but now he was putting a kettle on a Calor gas stove. 'I don't do much cooking here,' he said.

'What do you do?'

'Come over to think, away from everything. I've sorted out a few problems in this room.'

And she heard herself ask, 'Am I a problem?'

His voice was deep and slow, 'You could be the solution,' and she could almost believe she could mean that much to him, as she shut from her mind everything except what was happening to her here and now.

They drank the wine while they waited for the kettle to boil for coffee. Opened tins and ate with spoons. He told her about the lighthouse keepers so that she could 'see' them and imagine herself coming here with him, although if she had done it would have been as a babe in arms while he was in his teens.

Afterwards they went back to the duvet and made love slowly, feasting again, satisfying every need she had ever had, leaving her gloriously whole and marvellously fulfilled. She slept for a while then, and woke when he said her name, 'Millie. If we're walking back we should set off in about ten minutes. Otherwise we're here for another twelve hours or we signal for a boat.'

She didn't fancy the fuss that would cause. Everyone must know they had spent the night out here, the lights in the lighthouse would have told them that, but she didn't want a boat coming to pick them up nor having to face the abbey staff and guests looking ravished. She wanted a change of outfit and the chance to put on a little make-up, and she began to scramble for her scattered clothing.

Adam finished dressing. While she was getting into her oilskin coat he began to turn out the lamps, and she stood at the open door, in the shelter of the porch, as the lights went out behind her.

The moon was still out, silvering the rocks and the sand, and there were windows glowing in the abbey. Some lights would probably burn there all night, it was not dawn yet, almost everyone would still be sleeping.

As Adam closed the door and torchlight spilled down the rock steps at her feet, she said, 'So it wasn't the world's last night.'

'No.' He turned her towards him. 'But it might well be the first.'

She looked up into his face, and their eyes locked as though he could see into her soul. She said, 'Yes,' and pulled up her hood, shielding her eyes.

Tonight had been perfect. Nothing must spoil it, it had to stay perfect. She would have to wait until tomorrow before she could tell him . . .

CHAPTER SIX

THE way back was weird by moonlight. Drifting clouds made shifting shadows and the rocks took on strange shapes. Millie could think of nothing to say, and the noises of the sea seemed thunderous so that she was not sure she could make herself heard above it if her voice came out whispery. She hadn't the strength for shouting.

Adam guided her where the shingle was slippery with seaweed. His arm was around her most of the way, and when she looked at him he smiled at her. They were together against the buffeting wind, heading for the abbey that glimmered faintly on the clifftop. But she wondered if he felt as she did sometimes when the wind blew between them, as if she was slipping away from him.

She had to be tired; she hadn't had much sleep. The path up the cliff was hard to climb. Adam helped her to drag herself to the top and crossing the cloisters she stumbled against him more than once.

Inside the abbey, with the heavy door closed against the night outside, it was deadly quiet. But the shadows were in here with them. His face was dark, the stubble following his jawline was almost like a scar; and suddenly she was dizzy, as though she was losing her balance and her bearings.

'Come on, love, it's been a long night,' Adam said quietly.

It had been a lovely night but dawn would come, and when the sleepers woke and life started up again there were going to be some tremendous problems.

She stood, like a tired child, while he helped her out of her oilskin jacket and put it aside with his. Then she walked up the stairs and along the corridor, and at the door of her room she said, 'See you at breakfast.'

He said, 'Thank you,' and she quipped brightly and tritely,

'My pleasure.'

He had not planned to spend the rest of the night with her. She knew that now but she had not been so sure a moment before and she needed to be alone. He said goodnight and kissed her cheek, as if she *were* a sleepy child, then he left her and she went into her own bedroom.

A fire had been lit in the grate and burned down to ashes. The bedclothes were turned back, the white pillows and sheets looked inviting and she had to be tired. How long did she have? Three hours, four...

First a bath. She turned on taps and poured in something from one of the bottles. Undressed and slid into the warm water, looking down at herself as she went under the bubbles and came up sleek and dripping. She had a good healthy body, and last night she had felt like the sexiest woman in the world.

Well, she wasn't. She was all right but not spectacular, and that was the difference between them. Because he was spectacular, was Adam Schofield. He was filthy rich, staggeringly successful, and one

of the most sensual men she had ever come across,
a lover to set any woman on fire.

As the water lapped her she remembered the start
of the lovemaking, and how the heat had rippled
along her veins and arteries like a match set to a
powder keg. She had gone out of orbit, beyond any
pleasure she could ever have imagined.

'And we will some new pleasures prove,' the poet
had written, and the pleasures had been new, a
blinding revelation of what could happen to her
with Adam Schofield.

How it was for him she really did not know. He
was with her. He took her to the heights but she
might have been the only one on that trip not
knowing where she was going, seeing and hearing
nothing outside the cradle of his arms.

She got out of the bath, rubbing herself down
with a huge white fluffy towel. How would she face
Adam at breakfast? How would they go for the
rest of the day? And what—and she turned away
from the mirrored wall now because she couldn't
face herself even dimly in the steamed glass—was
she going to say to her brother?

She could never explain to Jack how she had let
the man he hated make love to her within days of
meeting him. And it wasn't just inexplicable, it was
so *stupid*, because she had started to like Adam.
He liked her and she had thought she might be able
to act the peacemaker in some way.

She hadn't worked out how but the idea had been
in her mind, and practically offering herself to him
was going to look like a ploy of the crudest kind.
Paying for a favour in advance. Making it so that
he owed her. Sexual blackmail. Of course she hadn't

planned it that way, she hadn't thought about anything, but it meant there was no chance of a rational
discussion.

Through the windows the night was still dark.
The clifftop was empty and she couldn't make out
the shape of the lighthouse against the black sky.
Perhaps there was no lighthouse. Perhaps tonight
had never happened and it had all been a dream.

Perhaps in four hours' time she would have some
idea how to unravel the tangle she had just made
of her life. She crawled into bed and sheer
exhaustion clobbered her so that she was asleep
almost at once.

Again she was woken by the woman with the
teatray. If the staff had known that the boss and
the girl he had brought down with him were in the
lighthouse for most of the night the woman showed
no surprise at finding her in her own bed now. This
must have happened before, other women with
Adam, and Millie felt a stab of jealousy that surprised her because she had never been bothered by
jealousy.

She sat up in bed, sipped her tea, clearing her
head. Last night's madness seemed farther away this
morning, as if it had happened a long time ago.
But then the memory of his long strong body beside
her was warm and close again as though they had
been together for years. And that wasn't just chemistry; that had to mean she was falling in love.

Adam hadn't understood either what lay beyond
the blinding sexual attraction. Something else, he
had said, something more.

She put the teacup very carefully back on the tray
on the bedside table, got up, washed and dressed.

She was in all manner of trouble but she was no
longer panicking. She was almost calm, as if she
had found the answer and it was so simple and obvious, it didn't need thinking about. It was just a
feeling that she and Adam could never hurt each
other, wrapping her round like a warm cloak.

She would take everything as it came and she
went downstairs prepared to do just that. There was
action down there. Not a holiday atmosphere any
more. Through the open door to the breakfast-room
perhaps, where some of the guests were sitting at
table, but Adam was on a phone in the office and
there was a man Millie hadn't seen before with him.

As she passed the door Adam saw her, smiled
and raised a hand, and she went on to the breakfast-
room where Monique, with an empty chair beside
her, gestured for Millie to join her. 'Here we go
again,' said Monique.

'Do we?' said Millie.

'Not us.' Monique gave a Gallic shrug. 'Our
menfolk. This time it is just Adam. Well, of course
all the time it is Adam but Peter does not go this
time.'

Adam, it seemed, was off to France, to Nancy,
as soon as a helicopter arrived to take him to an
airport. There was a panic and Monique rolled her
eyes at that—and he was leaving at once to deal
with it. 'How long?' Millie asked.

Another shrug, 'A few days.'

Millie's face fell, 'Oh!' she said.

She didn't want to stay here without him, and
perhaps she should be going home. Lots of little
responsibilities were waiting for her there. There
had to be trains, buses she could catch.

When Adam came looking for her she could hear the helicopter and she said, 'Monique's been telling me you have to go.'

'Sorry about this.' He sounded sorry; he looked it too. 'Peter will arrange transport for you. I'll be back Monday probably, I'll contact you.'

'Do that,' she said, 'I'm getting a lift home today.'

The charity organiser and her barrister husband were leaving after lunch, their home in Cheltenham not too far from Millie's. A detour was possible and Angela Cutler had offered as soon as Millie started asking about the train service.

She went out with Monique to watch the helicopter take off from a helicopter pad she hadn't seen before. There was still exploring to be done around here but only with Adam. He kissed her before he went, hands on her shoulders, looking into her face as if she still puzzled him, and her senses swam when his lips brushed hers so that she hung on to the lapels of his coat.

She loosed him first and managed a grin. 'Come back soon,' she said.

'I will.' His lips hardly moved and she nearly said, By the way, I know what it is between us. But she couldn't say that with Monique standing near, and the helicopter door open and the noise of its engine filling the air.

They waved it off and Millie turned smiling to Monique. 'Well, I had fun while it lasted,' and Peter Barkin's wife looked sympathetic.

'It was a shame. But it happens. Next week Peter is all over the country, here, there.' She made it sound as if he was doing one-night stands on a

dozen different stages, and perhaps he was. 'But
he comes home, and that is nice.'

'I'm sure it is,' said Millie.

'You ring me,' said Monique. 'We will have lunch
together and talk about our menfolk.'

'I'd like that,' said Millie, and knew that she
would not tell Jack.

They were expecting her at home. She phoned
before she left the abbey, reassuring her mother that
everything was fine and she was only coming back
early because Adam had had to go to France and
two of the guests were giving her a lift.

But Elena was prepared for another explanation.
Barbara was staying with her while Millie was away
and she was there tonight, smiling sadly and know-
ingly in the background. Flower had almost bowled
Millie over and Elena had hugged her and in the
drawing-room Elena asked, 'How did it go then?'

'I had a lovely time. It's a beautiful place, the
abbey, and everyone was smashing.'

'And then he went?'

'Had to.'

'And somebody else brought you back?'

'They live in Cheltenham.'

'Yes,' said Elena, exchanging glances with
Barbara, whose husband Millie guessed was still
cheating on her. 'Well, I did warn you he wouldn't
be around for long.'

'He has not dumped me,' said Millie, laughing
at the idea. She heard Barbara sigh,

'You can't tell me anything about men,' and
Millie said gaily,

'I wasn't going to.'

She looked at the phone as she passed it in the hall, carrying her case to her room, and willed it to ring. A call from Adam, checking she was home safe, would have shut them up in there. Two women with cheating husbands, if only her mother had known.

Adam didn't ring that night nor the next day. Millie didn't go into the *Sentinel* offices, she was on leave and Friday morning it seemed a good idea to change her bedroom wallpaper. That was a few years old and she was getting tired of it, so she drove out to a shop that sold super papers and paint and came back with all the things she needed.

She had done the home decorating for years; it was no hassle. She stripped off the old and waded into the new, and that meant she was busy all Friday, all Saturday, and too tired at night, she said, to do anything but stay around the house.

The phone rang several times but it was never Adam. Just after Sunday lunch it rang again, Millie jumped up to answer it but this time it was for Elena and Millie finished the washing up while her mother chattered in the hall. She had food packed in a bag to take along to the *Sandpiper* for Jack when he came, and for the first time she was not looking forward to seeing him.

One reason was obvious, but the other hit her as she let herself out of the house, calling to Flower and calling goodbye to her mother. Decorating her room had been her excuse for staying close to the phone all weekend, and she didn't want to leave the house now because of the hope that Adam might ring her.

She had been waiting to hear from Adam, every call had been a disappointment, and although she could tell herself how busy he was, that he had gone out to deal with an emergency, it still had to mean he was not thinking of her anywhere near as much as she was thinking of him.

She scurried around in the *Sandpiper*, turning on the little bottled gas fire, putting out the food, and when it was time for Jack to arrive she went out on to the towpath.

There wasn't another soul in sight. It was so cold and miserable that even the fishermen had stayed at home, and Flower was halfway across the bridge to the narrowboat when Millie shouted him back again. No welcome for them there until Adam came back, and even then she was not absolutely sure that she could stroll in uninvited.

Almost at once she saw Jack striding along, and called his name as she ran to him and he enveloped her in a bear hug, lifting her off her feet. 'Put me down, you idiot,' she giggled.

She *was* glad to see him. They went aboard the *Sandpiper* arm in arm, and inside he took off his coat and unravelled a scarf. 'Better in here,' he said. 'It's bitter out there.'

'Have something hot.' She had a kettle boiling, soup in a Thermos. Half a bottle of wine—he was driving back to London—and food laid out on the table.

He took a glass of wine, a couple of gulps, then he wanted to know, 'What's happened?'

'Just chat. Everybody liked him down there.'

'Well, they would, wouldn't they? His mates staying in his house.' His look of concern was for her. 'It must have been grim for you; I was sorry afterwards that I let you go. Did he come back here?'

She was pouring some soup into a bowl and filling a plate with quiche and salads for him. 'No, there was some sort of flap on. A helicopter came for him, he was making for Nancy in France.' Perhaps Jack knew about that.

He nodded as if it registered and asked, 'How did you get back?'

'I got a lift with a woman who's a big charity organiser. She said that Adam gives a lot to charity.'

Jack gave a hoot of laughter, 'Tax dodges.' Just what she had known he would say. 'Charity begins and finishes at home in Adam Schofield's book. He could never be a soft touch.'

Adam's touch had run through her like a sweet wildfire. She could feel it now and she began to talk fast. 'Jack, he likes me, he talked to me. Not about business, and nothing scandalous that you could use, but as if he trusted me. If I asked him to lay off whatever it is he's got on you maybe he would.'

Jack laughed again, if you could call it laughter. 'You say pretty-please and Schofield caves in?'

She hadn't much hope but she said, 'He might.'

'Not in my lifetime,' said Jack. 'Nor in yours. My only chance is something I can use against him and you might still come up with that. You are seeing him again?'

'Yes, but I think you could be wrong.' She was fiercely in earnest now. 'I've been with him and—we went out to a lighthouse just offshore from the abbey, just the two of us. We were there from low tide until low tide again, nearly all night, and I'm sure I know him better than—well, almost anybody.'

Jack's expression was of slowly dawning horror. 'My God, Millie, you're not falling for him?'

That was exactly what she was doing but she had to say, '*No*.'

'You couldn't be that stupid.' Jack was aghast, bringing out the ultimate disloyalty. 'You didn't *sleep* with him?'

There hadn't been much sleeping and she said, 'No,' again, lying, lying.

'That would be the end for you.' Even if he believed her he was still shaken. 'He uses everybody. Once he'd had you he'd be through with you. That would be my last chance blown out, but—oh, Millie, don't tell me you fancy that bastard.'

He was almost beside himself and she was the calmer, the stronger. That was what came of having to pretend so much—you learnt the knack of it, and right now she had to calm Jack down.

She said, 'We drank a bottle of wine and ate a meal, and I had a conducted tour round a little museum. He's a cool customer and so am I and I was not raped.'

That was true. Nothing had happened that she had not gloried in. She went on as Jack relaxed, relieved. 'All I'm saying is that I think he might be reasonable.'

Jack said, 'Sorry. Only you scared me. I wouldn't let you get into his clutches for the world. So, we'll be reasonable,' Jack sounded heavily sarcastic, 'How are you going to start, by telling him I'm your brother?'

If she pleaded for Jack she would have to explain why and she said slowly, 'He might keep quiet about it.'

'He wouldn't.' Jack was convinced of that. 'No, there's only one way we can deal with him. Now, tell me what they did talk about.' He sat down with his plate of food and there was no reason she should not hand over the tape. There was nothing on it but an account of a pleasant few days.

Yesterday she had talked about the wedding, who she had met there. Nothing that Jack or anyone else could use against Adam. She had finished dictating before the lighthouse because she couldn't talk about that to anyone.

Jack was wrong about Adam. He did not use his friends with no feeling for anyone but himself. Peter had been a friend for years and Peter was his fan for ever. Peter had tried to warn her but Peter only knew him 'better than most' and Millie knew him better than that, and Adam would be back tomorrow.

She sat with Jack and he told her about the deals his firm was handling and she told him silly things, like decorating her bedroom. She did ask, 'Just what *is* Adam threatening you with?' and Jack said irritably,

'I *told* you, a money transaction. But if it wasn't that it would be something else. He's gunning for me. He's a crook, Millie, as well as a bastard, and there's got to be something you can come up with now you've got him this far.'

'I haven't got him at all.' Adam would always be his own man. He hadn't phoned her—that showed he was not dependent on her.

'All right,' Jack said, 'we'll drop it for now, shall we?' He tapped the tape in his pocket. 'I'll go through this, and we'll take it from there.' He gave her a half-grin. 'I can't stay much longer; I've got to get back.'

She was always sorry to say goodbye but this time she didn't try to delay him. She stood on the deserted riverbank with Flower as her brother walked away, and waved back as he turned for a final wave at her.

Then she cleared up fast in the *Sandpiper*, throwing the debris and the plates and glasses for washing into her bag, and almost running home with Flower lolloping beside her.

'Is that you dear?' Elena called as always. Millie had said she was having a picnic with a friend on the boat. 'They've been a couple of calls for you.' Millie held her breath. 'Not from him,' said Elena.

Lyn, her colleague on the *Sentinel*, had phoned, and Maud was still after Millie, which meant Adam. 'I'll call Lyn back,' Millie told Elena, and went up to her room, sitting on the bed with her face in her hands.

She hadn't really expected Adam to ring in the last two hours but Jack had voiced her secret fear. Adam might have tired of her that quickly. Stranger things had happened. She felt Flower's head on her knee and looked down into watchful brown eyes. The dog sensed her distress, was waiting for one more little sign before he started howling in sympathy.

'Don't you dare,' she hissed.

She got up and got down to finishing wallpapering the last wall, so that she had a pretty new bedroom to sleep in that night, and maybe it was the smell of paint in the air that was giving her a headache. Her mother had been complaining about it all weekend.

They would all be waiting for her in the office this morning. She had called Lyn back last night but Lyn wouldn't be satisfied with the information she'd got. Three days with Adam Schofield would keep Millie's workmates gossiping for months, and although he'd said he would probably be back today Millie could tell them nothing about his future plans, either for the *Sentinel* or for herself.

Sally on Reception saw her first and called 'Hey,' as Millie scuttled for the stairs. 'Was it good in Cornwall?'

'It's good anywhere,' chortled a photographer who had walked in just behind Millie and Sally giggled while Millie said, 'There were ten of us staying in the Schofield residence. I was representing the peasants,' and went upstairs pretending to smile.

Probably back on Monday, Adam had said. But he was not back here. Or if he was he did not contact Millie. She handled the questions as best she could. Millie was a girl who didn't take life too seriously, they all knew that; and she had enough common sense not to have let it go to her head when Adam Schofield had taken notice of her.

Jeremy Warrald tried to put on a sympathetic act on Tuesday. 'Heard nothing from him since, haven't you? Well, you knew what you were letting yourself in for, but you're getting a rough deal there. I'm sorry about it Millie, but you know where your real friends are. We should never have split up.'

There hadn't been much of a relationship to split. They had dated a few times and then Millie had backed off and Jeremy had said it was her loss and taken what he was being offered elsewhere. But he still fancied Millie; he could see what Schofield saw in her. 'I'd be willing to give it another chance,' he said.

'Give *me* another chance?' Millie did her wide eyes. 'Ah, isn't that nice?'

Jeremy smiled quite smugly. She was laughing at him but she was worth waiting for, because even if Schofield hadn't done with her yet he was hardly staking a claim.

For Millie it was not nice at all. It was verging on the horrible after she rang Monique on Tuesday night. That seemed an obvious thing to do. Adam had thought he might be back on Monday and said he would contact her. She had heard nothing from him, but she had Monique's number and maybe Monique knew the news from France. She had seemed quite keen to keep in touch but as soon as Millie said, 'It's Millie Hands,' she heard a little gasp before Monique said, 'Hello, how are you?'

'Fine,' said Millie. 'I wonder, have you heard anything from Adam?'

'No.' But that was drawn out as if Monique was making it last because she didn't know what to say next.

Monique knew nothing. No news. No messages. Her charming lilting accent conveyed a brush-off that Millie would have had to been very thick-skinned not to recognise. When they'd parted, Monique had been on about having lunch together discussing their menfolk; now there was nothing at all she wanted to discuss with Millie. Between Thursday and Tuesday her attitude towards Millie had changed, from being warm and friendly to being implacably determined to chill Millie out.

Peter might have advised his wife against getting too matey with Millie but Monique was a lively lady. She would only be acting like this if there was more behind it than Peter counselling caution. To be chilled off by Monique the word must have come from Adam. She couldn't believe it, she *wouldn't* believe it, but until Adam got in touch there was no way she could know for sure.

Somehow the week dragged on, with no word. The state Millie was in it was a wonder that Flower didn't start howling and never stop, but somehow she managed to keep the dog quiet and everyone else fooled. She did her work, well. She acted her way through the long hours and when the phone rang for her in the office and at home she answered like an actress, hiding the sick stomach lurch of disappointment every time.

Her friends *were* fooled. It was only a week and nobody was saying he wouldn't call on Millie again, and she certainly wasn't breaking her heart about it. That was the general opinion, but one woman proved perceptive and sensitive and surprisingly kind.

On Friday Mrs Beale from the office switchboard, who could be relied on to hear the gossip before anyone else and who could spread it faster than anybody, caught Millie at the coffee machine with no one else near and said quietly, 'My friend who works at Alderson Towers has just told me Adam Schofield's booked in there tonight.'

Millie stretched her lips in a smile, trying to look as if she knew and failing. 'He'll be phoning you,' said Mrs Beale hopefully.

'Yes,' said Millie, not sure at all, and Mrs Beale suddenly looked motherly—although not like Millie's mother—and concerned.

Of course Adam might look Millie up but the whole office would be waiting for that as soon as they heard he was back in town. 'Nobody knows,' said Mrs Beale, adding, 'Nobody's business,' and Millie admitted everything by saying,

'Thank you.'

Most of the day she was in the magistrates' courts, covering speeding offences and minor misdemeanours. Nothing interesting enough to merit more than a few lines in the *Sentinel*, if that, so she had plenty of time to think.

He *might* phone her today, he might turn up this evening, but from Monique's attitude, and more than a week with no word at all, she knew she was pretty low on Adam Schofield's priorities. And if he didn't get in touch in the next twelve hours she could count him out of her life because she was surely out of his.

It hurt terribly. It couldn't be hurting more if she had been in love with him. She was not in love. She had been wrong there, it *was* only a physical infatuation, and she thanked her stars for that, but it did hurt.

There were no messages for her at the office and no phone calls in the evening. She watched television alone, Elena was out, and Millie sat through two hours' viewing with only the faintest idea what she was watching. When the phone did ring she nearly broke her neck, falling over Flower, to get to it. But it wasn't Adam.

Elena had said this morning how well the roses were lasting, but tonight the petals were falling, and tomorrow Amy would throw them away if Millie didn't.

The phone rang again and Maud was the last straw. Millie told her through gritted teeth that she had no idea when Adam would be free for a musical evening but he was tone-deaf anyway so she hardly thought it would be his scene. Then she slammed down the phone and swore at it.

He was not getting in touch with her and, until now, she had not known how to contact him. But she knew where he would be this evening, where he probably was now, and a week's frustration had her nerves stretched to screaming point.

If Adam was through with her he could damn well tell her so. And it would be no big deal. Whichever way you looked at it theirs had been a doomed relationship, so to know for sure it was finished should be a relief.

His car was in the hotel car park. Millie left Flower in hers and went to the reception desk and asked if Adam Schofield was here. Odds were he wouldn't be alone and that could be embarrassing, but her adrenalin was so charged up that she could have faced him in a crowd and still said her piece.

A receptionist rang through and said would she go up? She remembered the number, it was the same suite. She took the stairs, walked the same corridor, and knocked on the door. But in the seconds that followed the heat of her indignation subsided rapidly, leaving her chilled through and through, because how Adam greeted her, and what he had to say to her, suddenly seemed a matter of life and death.

CHAPTER SEVEN

ADAM opened the door and said, 'Hello,' his face expressionless, except perhaps for a faint weariness in the lift of an eyebrow or the quirk of the long mouth. But Millie knew that she was a nuisance, an intruder, and the chill settled in her bones.

She asked, 'Am I interrupting anything?' There might be someone else here. He could be in a business conference or entertaining friends. One thing was certain: he was not glad to see her.

He said, 'Yes,' and stood aside, 'but come in.'

He could hardly leave her standing outside the door but his voice had an edge of impatience and she should be saying, Then I won't bother you; and walking away. But she couldn't do that, and she stepped past him into the room.

There was no one else that she could see, although they could be in the bathroom or the bedroom, and her voice seemed remarkably normal considering the tightness in her throat. She would have expected to sound strangled as she said, 'You didn't ring.'

'Things have been hectic.' A good excuse, coming from the head of Schofield Enterprises for whom every day must be humming and buzzing, but Adam Schofield could have made the time to phone her if he had wanted to.

He didn't look as if he was finding life hectic. He looked relaxed and bored. He looked straight at her and didn't give a damn, and it helped feeling so cold that all her emotions were in deep freeze.

She said, 'I phoned Monique.'

She knew for sure now that Monique had been told Adam was distancing himself from Millie, which had to be in case Millie presumed too much from a one-night stand. Where did that line come from? It sounded Victorian... Sir, you presume too much...

A sick humour was twisting her lips, and she turned it into a wry joke. 'Monique was not too happy to hear from me either.'

'No?' He was not surprised, nor interested, and she gave a little shrug,

'It seems I got the wrong impression last week. I thought I was more important than I am.'

'Don't we all?' he said, and she thought, Not you. You think you've got clout enough to smash anything or anybody that stands in your way, and most of the time you have.

She had to get out of here. 'Sorry to have troubled you,' she said sweetly. 'Sorry the chemistry didn't come up to expectations.'

'On the contrary,' he drawled. 'The chemistry was amazing.' And she agreed with him as if they were discussing a film they had seen.

'I thought so; I could swear the tower shook and that had to be amazing. But now——' She actually smiled. 'Best forgotten?'

He had never taken his eyes off her for a moment, and when the phone rang like an alarm bell the narrowed eyes were so piercing that it was like having a dagger at her throat.

Then he turned to answer the phone and said, casually, 'I'll call you.'

'Do that,' she said.

In the car Flower whimpered all the way home, and when Millie let herself into the house the dog kept so close beside her that she bumped against him climbing the stairs. The television was still on in the drawing-room; that was because she hadn't bothered to switch it off, not because her mother was back.

It was early yet, and Elena would have called out if she had been here, and the house felt empty. Millie felt empty, drained of everything. She slipped off her coat and let it lie where it fell. Then she sat on the stool in front of the dressing-table, as her legs gave way, and stared at her reflection in the mirror with unseeing eyes.

She had made another mistake, haring after him to his hotel. She should have accepted that she had been the briefest of brief affairs. She had made herself a challenge at the start and sexual challenges would be a novelty for Adam Schofield. Only she wasn't a challenge so much as a pushover and, as Jack said, 'Once he'd had you he'd be through with you.'

An old story and there was nothing she could do about it, except pretend it hadn't mattered much for the sake of her pride. And because he was dangerous.

She had to have imagined it but just now, while the phone was ringing, she had thought he was angry enough to strike her. That was crazy, but it showed how worked up she was.

She sat with her feet tucked under her on the carpet, her arms around the only living creature who seemed to love her unquestioningly, and sobbed great silent sobs even when Flower was howling with her.

But when the dog reached the pitch that could be reaching the neighbours she had to soothe him down, and by the time Elena returned she saw nothing amiss in either Millie or Flower. She did ask, 'Any interesting phone calls?' but when Millie said,

'No, nothing,' she yawned and said she would be getting to bed. And would Millie keep her own bedroom door closed because the smell of the paint was making Elena quite bilious?

If her mother had looked harder and asked, 'What's the matter?' Millie might have told her that she was wretchedly unhappy. Not told her everything of course. No mention of Jack. Hearts didn't break, that was a romantic fiction, but a heart could ache so dreadfully that you wondered if it was breaking.

Talking might have helped Millie but Elena could see nothing wrong and Millie was no more alone than she had been for years. It was just that the loneliness seemed worse tonight. Her brother had been her confidant ever since they found each other, but she would get no sympathy from him over this.

If she was going through a little hell now, in Jack's eyes it was of her own making. He had told her the kind of man she was dealing with. She had been forewarned but she had carried on like a star-struck groupie.

She was glad her mother had not noticed how red her eyes were. Confiding in Elena would only have made matters worse.

She lay in bed in the silent house, with the dog on the rug beside the bed twitching in his sleep. Adam couldn't have made it plainer that he was through with her if he had hit her across the face. His message had been spelled for her loud and clear. And yet, something was wrong, off key, out of character.

She couldn't explain the gut feeling, that might be only a crazy hope, that this was not the end, that something else had to happen.

Saturday was the official day off for the *Sentinel* staff, although reporters and photographers often covered Saturday events. Today Millie went over to a small neighbouring town to see the Christmas lights switched on and chat to shoppers and traders. She spent the day there, buying some Christmas gifts herself, deliberately staying where the crowds were rather than going home.

When she did arrive home Elena came hurrying out as Millie's Fiesta drew up, and as Millie opened the car door Elena said, 'He phoned. Adam Schofield.'

For a moment Millie's spirits soared but immediately she sobered down. 'What did he want?' she asked.

'You,' said Elena, as if that was a silly question. 'He thought you didn't work on Saturdays. Anyhow, he's calling again.'

Elena was not sure about this, but Adam Schofield did have a reassuring and persuasive way with him, and she had found herself responding to his flattering enquiries about her well-being and telling him that Millie would be bound to be home no later than six o'clock.

She went indoors with Millie, conceding, 'He took his time phoning you but he must be very busy so I suppose you're lucky it was no longer.'

'Oh, I'm the lucky one,' said Millie.

...'I'll call you,' Adam told her last night. So, he was calling, so he must have something to say; and while Millie waited she took Flower out on the lawn and threw an old tennis ball for him to chase and retrieve. Exercising the dog and listening for the phone at the same time.

It rang at five minutes past six and Millie hurried in through the back door, but her mother beat her to it and twittered, 'Yes, you've got me again,' before she handed it over.

It was Adam and Elena was standing there, openly listening, so that Millie had to hide the fact that his voice made her heart lurch. She ran upstairs with the phone as he was asking, 'What are you doing this evening?' and waited until her bedroom door was closed before she let herself gasp,

'You're not saying you want to see me again?'

'Why not?'

It seemed incredible, but he was a good deal more sophisticated than she was. The lighthouse episode hadn't meant much to him and she must have convinced him that she had not considered it gave her any claims. She said, 'All right,' and he said,

'Half an hour?'

'Make it an hour, I've only just got in.' That sounded casual enough. Not as if she couldn't wait to see him.

She took the phone downstairs and replaced it. Her mother was still in the hall. 'That was a short call,' said Elena.

'We're going out.'

'Well, I suppose you know what you're doing by now,' said Elena.

I know what I'm not doing, thought Millie. Never again. What I'm doing will be platonic and wary, because when I tried it the other way I got a very rough awakening.

She took trouble with her appearance and when she heard the doorbell ring she didn't rush to answer it. Elena would probably be at the door first anyway, and Millie went on brushing her hair.

Her mother didn't call her so perhaps it was not Adam, but when she came out of her room she could hear voices from the studio. Her mother was showing him her father's paintings and he turned from one to smile at Millie.

She forced an answering smile and sauntered in, and knew she was still being a fool to herself because she would get no joy from being with him. It just made her miserable and this evening was going to be the last time.

Adam said all the right things about the paintings, and Elena looked at the unfinished self-portrait on the easel with misty eyes. 'We've kept everything just as it was, so that he could walk in and pick up a brush and finish this.'

No he could not. The brushes were rock-hard, the paints on the palette had set like concrete, but

Millie knew that her mother believed what she was saying. 'When I come in here I feel that he's still with me.' Then Elena gave a tremulous smile, 'Well, now you've seen my treasures I won't keep you any longer. Take care of my little girl, won't you?'

'For gawd's sake,' gasped Millie, and Adam said gravely,

'Of course.'

As they got into the car Millie said, 'You didn't think much of them, did you?'

'No,' he said. She knew about his collection; she had seen the pictures at the abbey. She knew her father's work couldn't compare with them, but Adam had admired all the paintings for Elena, and Millie couldn't have said how she knew what his opinion really was. But now he had admitted it so bluntly that she felt that he might have spared her feelings too.

She said tartly, 'Good thing we're not trying to sell them to you, although you could always call it charity and charge it somehow.' Then she went on quickly, before he could ask what she meant by that, 'The emergency in Nancy was cleared up, was it?'

'Yes.'

Silly question. When Adam Schofield handled an emergency it was well and truly dealt with. She said, 'By the way, Maud phoned again. Twice, actually. Last time was last night and I told her what you told me to tell her, that you were tone-deaf and never went to musical evenings.'

'Quite right,' he said. 'And I got another call from the couple who are anxious to give us dinner. The Forrests. That's where we're going to now.'

There was no escape. No excuse would get her out of this at this stage. Unless she said, I was the one who did for his political career. That weekend with the model might have come out later but I doubt it. It was only the whisper of a rumour when it reached me, and I told Jack and Jack moved mountains to find her and get her talking...

If Adam knew that he wouldn't let her near Rosemary and David, and it was too late now to wish she had said no to coming out with him this evening. She had to say that where they were going was fine by her, and how kind it was of them to invite her too; and then pretend to listen to the radio for the rest of the journey, dreading what was waiting for her.

The Forrests' house was large and detached in a tree-lined avenue. The engineering works had weathered the recession and they seemed a happy family. Rosemary and David came hurrying out when Adam's car drew up and their delighted welcome included Millie.

Getting Adam Schofield here had been some-thing of a coup for David Forrest. Schofield Enterprises were big business, but there was friendship too. The men liked each other, and a boy in the hall and a girl with bright carroty hair leaning over the banisters, were both grinning broadly.

'They're off to a pop concert,' said Rosemary, sounding like an anxious mum.

'We wouldn't have gone if we'd known you were coming,' said the girl.

'Only we've got tickets,' said the boy. 'And it's the Poppy Shocks.'

'No contest,' said Adam.

The boy had been sixteen, and the girl fourteen, a year ago when the scandal broke. Millie had felt sorry for them, and their mother. She knew how she had felt when she learned that her own father was a cheat, but they seemed to have weathered this storm too.

It was awful, taking their hospitality, eating their food, drinking their wine, when she had plotted what must have been their darkest hours. She had never sat through a more uncomfortable meal, and it did not get easier when Rosemary said that David had been approached about his name going back some time on the prospective parliamentary candidates' list.

'What do you think?' she asked Adam.

'What does David think?' said Adam.

David looked glum. 'I don't think so.' He grinned wryly. 'I'd be a lost cause before they started.'

'No, you wouldn't,' said his wife, and she refilled his wine glass and raised hers so that they were toasting each other.

Millie thought, she loves him and he loves her. There's a lot of love in this house so how did it happen?

When Rosemary left the dining-room to fetch the sweet out of the kitchen David said, 'It's not on. I'd have that little rat Jack Perry coming out of the sewers again.'

'I think you would,' Adam agreed, and Millie felt her face go white and cold. She wanted to speak up for Jack. She wanted to defend him but David was speaking to Adam.

'You could deal with him. Sharon Ward was a set-up. And what was printed about me was a load of garbage but I was with the girl, I couldn't deny that, and that was all the muckrakers needed.'

He looked across at Millie, 'Sorry, Millie, I know you don't go in for that kind of journalism on the *Sentinel.*'

She said, 'We aim to please,' trotting out a cliché and feeling sick, and Rosemary came back with a chocolate whisky cake which she said was a recipe of her Irish grandmother's but which David said she had got out of a packet.

It was like no packet pudding Millie had ever seen. Rosemary seemed to be a superb cook. The meal was marvellous, only it tasted like ashes in Millie's mouth; and her dining companions were good company. David had a dry humour, Rosemary could tell a hilariously risqué story and Adam had them all helpless with laughter.

Millie laughed, although she felt she ought to be crying, and several times when she *was* laughing she looked around and thought, I'm a traitor here. And then a shadow fell across her again.

When she thanked them, as she and Adam took their leave, it was a lie to say how much she had enjoyed herself. She should have done. It was no fault of her hosts that she hadn't been able to relax for a moment. They couldn't have been kinder. Or nicer.

'They are so nice,' she murmured, waving goodbye to the two who stood in their open doorway, the man's arm around his wife's shoulders.

'They are,' he said.

'Then why——' she ran her tongue between her dry lips ' —why did he go off with that girl? How could he do something as awful as that to Rosemary?'

They were out on the main road. Not meeting much traffic, Adam was driving fast and looking straight ahead. His voice was flat and curt. 'Cut out the dramatics. The sex-slave rubbish, that was fantasy.'

'How do you know?'

'That isn't David. They'd had a row, they're a volatile pair, and he made a fool of himself. Rosemary knew. She'd given him hell and they'd put it behind them when the story broke. But what was printed and what happened were poles apart.'

She said slowly, 'I see.' David had still cheated but if Rosemary had forgiven him, and the children had not been harmed, perhaps Millie should not have listened to the whispers.

'If you do see,' said Adam, 'it's been an instructive evening for both of us.' And he didn't sound as if he was talking about the recipe for the whisky cake that Rosemary had written out for her. 'I've got to hand it to you,' he said. 'You surprised me.'

'How?'

'You never flinched.' She was holding her breath now, gripping her hands together tighter and tighter as he went on, 'Peter Barkin has a soft spot for narrowboats. On Sunday afternoon he was in this area so he came over to look over Al's boat. He looked out when you shouted to the dog and he saw your very affectionate meeting with Jack Perry.'

She couldn't get a word out, but he reacted as if she had denied it. 'Oh, Peter knows Perry, he made no mistake, and that answered a few questions.'

She was still silent and rigid. 'Like the name of your lover,' Adam drawled. 'And why you were keeping him under wraps. Not a man to be proud of. Your workmates might not be top-flight journalists but they probably have ethics, and Perry gives even the gutter Press a bad name.'

She found a voice then. 'He has ethics. He cares about the truth. He shows up the cheats.'

'Cheats?' His contempt was lashing. 'That's rich, coming from you. You're the most accomplished cheat I've ever come across, and I'm mixing with experts. As for the truth, he wrote the bloody scenario for Sharon Ward himself and went to her with it.'

'No!'

'*Yes*. The house was empty. She wasn't in it and neither was I. The whole thing was fiction. He gambled and lost; that's why he settled out of court.'

'I don't believe you.' She wanted to scream but she could hardly whisper and he went relentlessly on.

'That doesn't worry me. What does stick in my guts is that you both set out to get me and you almost did. I've heard of sleeping your way to the top but you were sleeping your way to the dregs. Does he know you went that far? It wouldn't surprise me; he's one of nature's——'

'*No!*' She did scream then. She couldn't let him say that about Jack. 'He knew nothing about the lighthouse. He'd go mad if he did. And he isn't my lover, he's my brother.'

'Ha!' He gave a hoot of derision. 'Not that old chestnut.' And everything was rushing at her, all the lies, and deceptions, like the road burning up beneath their tyres and the hedgerows hurtling past the windows.

She moaned, 'You're going too fast.' In every way, she meant, but he brought the car to a dead halt that sent her lurching forward in her seatbelt. Then he leaned across her and opened her door,

'Get out,' he said. She was getting out as soon as her shaking fingers freed her from the belt. 'You did break the David Forrest story?' She nodded. He'd guessed anyway; that was why they were there tonight. 'How many more?'

Not that many. Nothing very dramatic, and right now she was too confused even to remember the details. It was all a horrible mess. Her shoulders shivered on a shrug as she still fumbled with the belt.

'I do advise you to get out.' And now his voice was soft and terrifying. 'Because if you don't I could half kill you. You may think it would be worth it to get another juicy scoop for Jack-the-lad, but make your mind up quickly.' And she almost fell out on the grass verge, slithering down the shallow ditch as the car drew away at speed.

She had one small scrap of luck that night. Within minutes a car drew up alongside as she stumbled on, and a middle-aged woman wound down the window and said 'Millie Hands?' as if she couldn't believe her eyes.

It was someone Millie knew. Not all that well. She probably hadn't heard about the Adam Schofield affair, but she was shocked to find someone who was a girl in her eyes wandering along dark country lanes this time of night.

Millie climbed gratefully into the back seat and the husband started the car up again while the wife wanted to know, 'What *are* you doing out here?'

Millie hadn't the wits to invent an excuse. She said, 'I had an argument with the man who was driving me and I got out of his car.' The woman tutted but let it go at that. She would talk, of course. This would get around—and Millie could not have cared less.

They took her all the way home and, putting her off at her gate, the woman said, 'I don't know, young folk do take chances these days.'

'Yes,' said Millie. 'Well, thank you.'

She had to phone Jack. She had to tell him what had happened. Flower came bounding at her and her mother called from upstairs, 'Is that you, dear?'

'Yes.' Millie took the phone up with her. As she passed her mother's bedroom door Elena asked, 'Did you have a nice time?'

'Yes,' said Millie, and this time even Elena caught something not quite right in her voice. But, being Elena, she sighed and decided to leave it till morning.

In her bedroom, with the door closed, Millie tapped Jack's number. When he answered she said, 'Millie here,' and he said,

'Hold on,' and to somebody else, 'This won't take a moment.'

Jack had numerous girlfriends. He was getting out of earshot of whoever was in his flat with him because Millie heard a door close before he said 'Hello' again.

She gave it to him straight. 'Adam knows I know you. Peter Barkin saw us meeting on Sunday and going into the *Sandpiper*.' And she heard Jack wince.

'Ouch! Where was he?' The joke was desperate. 'Up a tree?'

'On a boat.'

'Were they keeping tabs on you?'

'No, it was just bad luck.'

'That's that, then.' He was rueful but resigned. 'Schofield and his friends won't be telling you any more little secrets.'

She had learned no secrets; all she had learned was a bitter lesson. 'That's not quite all. I told him you were my brother.'

'You did?' That surprised him.

'He didn't believe me. He thinks we're lovers.'

'*What*?'

'Remember I told him I was in love and I didn't play around, I only wanted friends? Well, now I want him to know you're my brother. I don't want him to think I was plotting against him with a lover.'

'Why not?' Jack's voice was suddenly sharp.

'He thinks badly enough of me as it is. Somehow this makes it even worse.'

'Why should you care what he thinks?'

'I just do.'

'You have fallen for him, haven't you?' How could she deny it when she had as good as admitted it? 'Now listen to me, Millie,' Jack would have been shouting at her if there hadn't been someone else in the flat. As it was his voice came out hoarse with anger. 'I care about you, I care what happens to you, and I wouldn't do a thing to square you with Schofield. If he knows you're my sister he won't have much time for you but if he thinks we're lovers he wouldn't touch you with a bargepole. And if anybody asks me that is what we are. Or have been.'

She gasped, 'That is obscene.'

'That is a lie,' said Jack, 'but you'll never prove it, and if I can't get Schofield any other way that ought to knock some of the starch out of the arrogant bastard.'

He was not thinking about Millie; he was not concerned for her. His spite against Adam was venomous enough to make him forget even his own interests, and she reminded him, 'What about this fraud charge he's holding against you? If you'd got an enemy before, what do you think this is going to do?'

'I'll take my chance on that,' Jack snarled, and Millie pressed the button, cutting off the connection.

Now she had nobody. Her brother had turned against her too, and she wondered if he had ever really cared about her. As for Adam, there was no hope at all, and that was destroying her. Her head was throbbing agonisingly and she went to the window, opening it to let in the cool air.

Beyond the light from this window, falling on the lawn, the trees and the riverbank were all in darkness. But she remembered looking out from the window in the abbey and seeing Adam walking on the lawns below, and for a moment she could almost imagine that if she ran down now she would find him waiting for her.

No shadow moved. There was nobody there. When she had met him by moonlight in the cloisters she should have told him everything, all about Jack. But even then it would have been too late. Right from the beginning it had been too late.

CHAPTER EIGHT

WHEN Millie woke next morning her head was still aching. Her troubled sleep had done her no good at all, and it was as well it was Sunday because she didn't think she could have got through a day at work—especially if anyone started asking questions—without cracking up.

That would be the end. She would never live it down. And she couldn't handle phone calls either, or friends dropping in. She would clear off for a day alone and lick her wounds, or whatever you were supposed to do with a deep hurt to dull it enough to hide it.

No Amy on Sundays; no Ben in the garden either. Even during the winter Ben pottered around most days, and Amy had started work here as a girl. She was well over sixty now, still living with her retired schoolteacher sister, still coming here every weekday.

But on Sunday morning there was only Millie and her mother, and Elena came down in a pale blue negligee, looking wan and heavy-eyed. 'I hardly slept at all last night,' she complained. 'I had to take one of my pills. That smell of paint is really too much; I'll have to go out for lunch.'

The small area Millie had painted was odour-free by now and Millie knew, if her mother did not, that this was Elena's way of avoiding trouble. Millie's date last night had gone wrong and Elena could not

handle bad news. She could give advice, but she
shrank from any crises or confrontations that might
affect her personally. If Millie had been chirpier
this morning Elena would have brightened up too,
but Millie was too wretched to pretend she was
happy.

So Elena blamed the new paintwork in Millie's
bedroom and rang up an old bachelor friend who
was always ready to escort her anywhere, and Millie
said she was off too and wouldn't be home till
evening.

Elena asked no questions. Millie left before her
mother did, and knew that Elena would spend the
next hour or so making herself look as lovely and
almost as young as the painting that hung over the
mantelpiece.

Millie loved her, and was proud of her. All
Millie's life friends had been saying, 'Isn't your
mother beautiful?' But although Elena sometimes
pretended that Millie was sixteen still, it was she
who was the child and had to be protected. Millie
couldn't break down. If she did, her mother would
fall apart. So she had to get through today, and
tomorrow, and before long she must start
pretending that everything was all right again;
although this morning she could not see her way
ahead at all.

She climbed into the car with Flower and headed
out of town, and was half an hour down the
motorway, in the fast lane with her foot down,
before she decided she might as well make for the
coast.

Not Cornwall. She didn't think she would ever
want to see Cornwall again. But the nearest seaside

town should be as good as anywhere else. This time of year there wouldn't be many holidaymakers, and she could walk herself weary without the risk of meeting somebody who knew her and wanted to talk to her.

The day went as she had hoped. Most of the hotels, large and small, were closed. Streets were almost empty. She could have parked anywhere and a cold wind swept the deserted beaches. She and Flower walked for miles, the dog high on sea air, leaping and racing, barking the waves back, his coat as shiny as a seal's from the spray.

Millie looked a bit like a seal herself, her hair dark and wet from the flurries of rain that swooshed in on the wind. She bought cooked food from a supermarket where she seemed to be the only customer and fed most of it to the dog, sitting in the open car in a deserted cove while the seagulls screamed around them.

Physically it was an exhausting day. The dog slept on the way home and Millie could feel a heaviness in her limbs that meant she had raced herself almost to a standstill. But she hadn't done much towards clearing her mind. She had got through today by avoiding everyone but she had no idea how she was going to cope with tomorrow.

Her mother had company. There were a couple of cars outside, and voices reached Millie as she entered the house. She looked in the drawing-room and said, 'Hello,' recognising the familiar faces of her mother's friends.

'Have a nice time?' Elena called across, and Millie said,

'So-so,' because that was as far as she could go right now.

She ran a hot bath, washing the stickiness off her skin and out of her hair, then got into bed, still hearing the voices below.

It was lateish when the visitors left and Elena came upstairs almost at once, but she didn't open Millie's door. She would be telling herself Millie was asleep and she didn't want to disturb her, but it didn't surprise Millie.

These nights there seemed no way Millie could persuade Flower to sleep downstairs; the dog had taken up permanent guard duty on her bedside rug. One who couldn't face up to unhappiness and one who wouldn't keep away. It was something to have some sympathy, if it was only from a dog. And he kept Millie from snivelling into her pillow because at the first sob he would be howling.

So Millie lay dry-eyed and hoped that if Elena was taking a sleeping pill again tonight she would stop at one. But they were low-strength, and she had been using them for little upsets for years and, so far, this would only be a little upset for her.

Millie had to see it stayed that way for her mother. For herself it was a disaster that was crushing the life out of her, as though she had been battered into a corner and left too bruised to fight.

Some time she would fight. When she was healthy again she would see Adam again. God knew what she would say to him, how she could explain, but somehow she must, because she could not live the rest of her life like this.

*   *   *

Millie was hardly inside the kitchen next morning before Amy was demanding, 'You all right?' and that was after Millie had put on mascara and blusher.

'Why shouldn't I be?' said Millie. She was on time for getting to work but had no time for talking, and there was nothing she wanted to talk about, not even to Amy, who waited a moment and then went on laying the table for Elena's breakfast.

Millie decided not to bother with coffee or anything else. She was walking to the office this morning—she would be in town all day—and she hoped the exercise would put a healthier colour in her cheeks and brighten her eyes before she had to face her workmates. Of course she was not all right, but she was not discussing why not with anybody.

On the surface it was a normal day for Millie. Covering the stories that had her name by them in the diary, she was out of the office most of the day; and when she was in she didn't know if anyone had heard that somebody had picked her up well out of town and well after midnight on Saturday, because she had had a row with a man in a car.

Nobody brought that up. There was something about Millie today that held them off. They were not a particularly sensitive bunch but they did get the impression that being too nosy round Millie right now might get a very sharp reaction. They might ask each other, 'What's going on with Millie?' but Millie herself they did not ask.

That evening Elena's desertion was quite a relief too. Elena met her in the hall as Flower danced around her and asked, 'Had a good day, dear?'

'Not bad,' said Millie. She did smile but it wasn't a brilliant effort and her mother said,

'I had a phone call from Stella Reynolds today.' Another old friend. 'She was saying how long it is since we saw each other. They want me to go and stay with them for a few days.'

It probably had happened that way. Elena often took holidays, often visited friends or had them staying here. Although Millie wouldn't have put it past her to have made the phone call herself, knowing there was always an open invitation for her.

She would be safe and happy at her friends'; the Reynoldses had a pleasant social life, and Millie felt as though they had taken a burden off her shoulders, like someone offering to mind a child when there was a bereavement in the home. She would find it easier being alone herself, and by the time her mother returned she might have pulled herself together.

Amy understood how Elena's mind worked. Next morning, with Elena not up yet, and Millie gulping down coffee in the kitchen, Amy said, 'Your mother's off for a few days, then?'

'To Stella's,' said Millie.

Amy knew all their friends. She said, 'I suppose you couldn't put a brighter face on things?' and Millie almost told her about Adam. But if she did start talking she might not be able to stop.

She said, 'Not just yet I can't,' and Amy nodded, biding her time.

Millie spent all her working hours that day at a DIY exhibition. The *Sentinel* was getting a lot of advertising revenue out of this and giving it plenty of coverage, so Millie's day was filled and she stayed with it doggedly. Work kept her from thinking about anything else, and she was glad that her mother would not be waiting for her when she got back home.

It had been tough enough pretending all day long; when she returned to an empty house she could give way a little and perhaps start to plan what she was going to do next.

There were lights on in the hall. Amy usually went home around five and a light was always left burning for Flower, who came to greet Millie as usual. But the kitchen door was open and Amy appeared in the doorway. 'I stayed to see you ate something,' said Amy.

She often cooked the evening meal and left it prepared when she left, but tonight she was ladling soup into a bowl and there was a savoury smell from the oven.

Millie had had a sandwich for lunch and only eaten half of that but she was not hungry. She might get the soup down but heavier food was beyond her, although, having put the bowl on the table, Amy pulled out a chair and settled herself as if she was preparing to watch Millie eat a hearty meal.

'They came for your mother,' she said.

So Elena's friends had collected her and Millie was sure she had gone off smiling, and she would be phoning her daughter but she would not be back until the end of the week at least. 'And somebody phoned about half an hour ago,' said Amy. 'Said he'd ring again but it would have to be lateish because he's out till then. Name of Jack.'

A little spasm in Millie's throat made her gulp, but Amy was already fixing her with beady eyes. 'Haven't heard about him before, have we?' said Amy. 'So who is this Jack when he's at home?'

Millie and Elena were as close to Amy as her own sister. Millie had always run to Amy with childish cuts and bruises. It was Amy who had bathed and bandaged and comforted, and Amy was entitled to a straight answer now. So Millie said, 'Would it surprise you if I told you he was my brother?'

Amy's face went blank. Then she gave a little grimace that asked if this was some daft joke. But Millie was not smiling and Amy asked, 'How old is he?'

'Two years older than me.'

'Well, he can't be your mother's. Your father's?' Millie was astonished that Amy seemed to be considering this, and even more surprised when Amy nodded and said, 'Mmm,' latching on to something.

'Did you know?' Amy knew something. The news was not a complete shock to her.

'Not about the lad,' said Amy. 'I knew about her. The mother she'd be, I reckon. Is she still around?'

Gasping, Millie managed to get out, 'She died. There were letters. Jack didn't know until then and he got in touch with me,' and as Amy went on nodding she croaked, 'Who else knows?'

'Nobody but Essie,' said Amy calmly. Esther was her sister and no more of a gossip than Amy was. 'He told me because I knew something was going on and he told me it was finished. He knew I wouldn't be spreading scandal. Your mother couldn't have stood it, even when she was a girl,' said Amy as if she was explaining that to Millie, who said wryly,

'I know she couldn't.'

'Of course you do,' said Amy. 'We both know the way she is.' And the old woman and the young woman looked at each other in mutual understanding. 'So how long ago did this lad turn up?'

'Two years ago.'

'What's he like?'

How could Millie describe Jack? He was a rat, but a likeable rat if there was such a thing. She said drily, 'A Jack-the-lad—do you know what that means?' and Amy said scornfully,

'Of course I know what it means. There've always been Jack-the-lads. Your father was one.'

Talking like this was helping. Millie knew now that she could have confided in Amy before, but if she had done Amy would have disapproved of Jack's lifestyle and certainly of Millie's involvement in it. They were not likely to like each other and Millie said, 'I'm glad you know, but I don't think you'll be meeting him.'

That was a safe bet. Millie did not want to see her brother herself for a long time, and when he phoned again tonight she would tell him.

'I don't want to see him.' Amy was emphatic about that. 'You keep him away. We can't have him turning up here. She'd be cadging a world tour with somebody after that; we'd be lucky if we ever got her back home again.' And that gave Millie her first real smile in days.

'That's it, then, is it?' asked Amy.

'Don't you think it's enough to be going on with?'

'He doesn't seem to have bothered you overmuch for two years, so what's the trouble now?'

Millie stirred her cooling soup and looking down into the bowl, pleaded, 'Would you mind if we left the rest till tomorrow? Suddenly I'm awfully tired; I seem to be all talked out.'

The spoon in her fingers was heavy as lead and she could hardly raise her head. Amy stood up and took down her coat from the hook behind the kitchen door. 'Early night for you,' she said, brisk as a nanny. 'Finish your soup and there's a pie in the oven. Now, you will eat it?'

'I will,' Millie promised.

'See you in the morning.' Amy buttoned herself into her coat, peering anxiously at Millie. 'And you will be all right?'

'Of course I will.' Millie teased, 'Don't worry, I'm not going to raid the sleeping pills.'

'She'll have taken them with her,' Amy chuckled. 'And I know you wouldn't be bothering with them; you're a good sensible girl.'

No, I'm not, Millie thought, I'm a wild one. And if I should tell you about Adam tomorrow you would go on loving me but you would be changing your mind about me being good or sensible.

After Amy left she finished the lukewarm soup and took jacket potatoes and a steak and kidney pie out of the oven. She salted and buttered the potatoes, eating some of them. Most of the pie she fed to Flower but she was almost keeping her promise to Amy.

She was less weary than she had thought, less inclined to have that early night, lying in bed alone, waiting to fall asleep. Perhaps it was just that she hadn't wanted to talk to Amy any more because it would have meant telling her about Adam.

She could discuss Jack fairly calmly, especially as Amy knew half the secret already. But it would be different with Adam. The moment she said his name she would choke up and her fragile self-control would crumble.

She would say something like, 'I love him terribly and he thinks I'm rubbish, and nothing is going to change his mind because I have been lying and cheating from the very first time we met.'

She said that to herself, aloud, gathering up the dishes and putting them in the sink. 'I could go along to the narrowboat,' she said. 'If there's smoke coming out of the chimney he might be there.'

Or Peter Barkin might, the man who liked narrowboats and who had seen her meeting Jack, and told Adam. And told his wife, who had been shocked and sickened. Millie could no more knock on the narrowboat door than she could phone Monique again. If Adam opened a door he would look at her as if he hated her and she couldn't endure that again.

Some time, next week perhaps or next month, she would write to Adam. Just, Sorry, please let us talk, Millie. He wouldn't answer but if he did what could she say? She walked around, talking in her head, pretending Adam was here, ready to listen to her and believe in her.

She dug the blue folder out of her undies drawer because she had to get rid of all Jack's briefings, and back in the kitchen she dropped pages on to the red-hot coals of the Aga stove. As she had burned the letters and the sketch and the photograph that Jack had brought with him the day he had said, 'I think I'm your brother.'

She was keeping the photograph of Adam, with Peter Barkin and the girl called Sharon, because it was a photograph of Adam and she couldn't watch the flames curl up around it. Not that she needed a photograph. She could see him all the time. She could feel him in every quivering nerve, as strongly as she had when he almost touched her at the beginning, his fingers skirting the outline of her face, nearly brushing her mouth. 'You feel it too, don't you?' he had said.

She had moaned, then turned away and started the lying when she should have believed what her heart was telling her, that this was a miracle in waiting. The dog barked and the doorbell rang and she went to answer it with her head spinning.

Adam stood there. For a moment she thought, I have flipped, I've gone crazy, I *am* seeing him everywhere; and she actually blinked as if the tall figure might turn into somebody else.

When it didn't—real and solid and six foot three, it was still Adam—she croaked, 'This is a surprise.'

'May I come in?' he said.

'Of course, of course.' The kitchen door was open and she went through it blindly.

Little flames were still leaping over the torn-up pages and she hooked the hob cover back, shutting them off. Then she slipped the photograph into the nearest dresser drawer, all the time talking jerkily. 'Do excuse the mess—I shouldn't be bringing you into the kitchen, should I? Can I get you anything? A drink? A good strong coffee?'

He said, 'Millie, do shut up,' and sat down at the table. 'Come and sit down,' he said as if they were in his office, and she took the chair opposite.

There was a long envelope between them. It lay on the table beside the empty blue folder. If Adam had arrived a few minutes earlier she would probably still have brought him in here, and the dossier would have been lying there waiting for him.

That proved that her mind wasn't working. She must calm down. She pressed her lips together, gripping her hands tightly on her lap, and stared at the white envelope because she couldn't look at Adam.

He said, 'This arrived at my London office this morning.'

'What is it?'

'From Jack Perry.'

She had guessed that. 'What does he say?' She watched him take out the letter, and watching his hands was almost as bad as staring into his face, meeting his eyes.

He pushed the sheets of paper across to her and she shoved them away and said, 'Tell me what he says.' She needed it summed up as briefly as possible. There were two typewritten single-spaced pages and she didn't think she could read what Jack had written about her to Adam.

Adam said, 'That you have been acting as an investigative reporter for his firm and you've been the source of some good stories. Details enclosed. When I took you down to Cornwall you were working for him, taping reports of conversations. But——' his voice had been detached and incisive, but this he was finding amusing '—he considers your conduct legitimate tactics and he hopes I won't take advantage, as the owner of the paper you're supposed to be working for, to fire you.'

The cheek of that jerked her up in her chair, and got her gasping, '*What*?'

'And,' said Adam, 'he says that you and he are very close friends.'

She said furiously, 'We are not close friends, if it means lovers, which it does. He is my brother.'

'Is that a fact?'

'It doesn't help a lot, it doesn't make any difference, but it is a fact.'

'Nobody mentioned this before.'

'Nobody *knows*.' This was sounding like another lie. 'He turned up with proof he'd found after his mother died, but he let me burn it because it would have killed my mother. He was born the first year of their marriage and—well, you saw her—that studio upstairs is a shrine; she worships the memory of my father. And she's so fragile, she can't face trouble.' Millie almost laughed. 'She's bolted now. She's away for a few days because I'm depressed and depression in the house always makes her ill.

'She mustn't know, and Jack said all right, he wasn't telling anybody, and there is no proof at all.' Even with Amy and Essie there was no hard proof, and Millie said desperately, 'Our eyes are a bit alike but nothing too striking and he's going to deny it. He doesn't want me to lose my job, very caring that is of him I must say, but this twist to the tale seems to appeal to his warped sense of humour.'

Her torrent of words dried up and Adam said laconically, 'I wouldn't believe Jack Perry if he told me the time. So, he's your brother,' and she couldn't believe that he believed her. She started to say thank you when he went on, 'But why did you do his dirty work for him?'

This she could explain. 'Because my father cheated. I'd thought he was wonderful until then, just as my mother does, and Jack's contacts seemed a way of getting back at hypocrites like him.'

'Perhaps. But why target me? I've never been a hypocrite.' He sat back in his chair, elbow on the table and chin in hand. 'The Sharon Ward settlement rankled, I suppose.'

'You nearly bankrupted Jack.'

'He deserved it.'

'He doesn't think so.'

'Oh, yes, he did, he knew he did. But I'm not surprised to hear he's got a king-size chip on his shoulder. So when you told him I was attracted to you—which you obviously did—he thought that put you in a position to get insider information?' She nodded miserably. 'And that's how it started, but why did you go on with it? Right from the beginning there was something between us but you never let up. What kept you grubbing around for something you could use against me?'

Her cheeks were burning and her excuse was wretched, although at the time she had felt she had no choice. She mumbled, 'He was protecting himself, against what you were going to do to him. He needed something he could threaten you with before you—sent him to gaol, he said.'

She looked up pleadingly and met a quizzically raised eyebrow. 'Go on,' Adam said gently.

'You do have something against him, don't you?' Money matters, Jack had said. He had been vague, just holding the threat of devastating disclosures over her. Her voice rose shrilly. 'You are gunning for him?'

Adam didn't laugh but he nearly did. 'He flatters himself. I've never bothered with putting Jack Perry out of business. I suppose I could start if you feel he expects it.'

He wasn't hiding the smile now and she was appalled. She had made such an idiot of herself again. There was no threat. Jack was in no danger from Adam. He had told her that to keep her working for him against Adam, and if she had found out anything harmful she just might have run to Jack with it.

She wailed, 'He lied to me.'

'Does that surprise you?' said Adam.

It shouldn't. Jack would consider it 'legitimate tactics' and her lips twisted as she tried to stop them trembling.

'So if it isn't Jack Perry,' he said, 'who is this secret lover of yours?'

'That was my lie.' That silly game was over. 'I thought it would keep things platonic between us.'

His eyes gleamed with laughter. 'Didn't do much good, did it?' And suddenly her trembling lips were smiling, because he didn't hate her and it was as if she had come out of a dark tunnel into the sunshine. She could even joke,

'Only because I thought it was the world's last night,' and they laughed together and she had never thought they would do that again. 'Are you going to sack me?'

'Possibly.' He wouldn't but it didn't matter.

'It doesn't worry you what happens to me?'

'Now there,' he said, 'we hit bedrock, because it worries me a great deal.' She leaned forward, looking into his face, his words soaking into her like sunshine. 'Five minutes after I'd thrown you out of my car and you'd landed in the ditch I remembered that you're accident-prone.'

'No, I'm not,' she murmured.

'I've got my own opinion there—but I went back for you.' And she thought that was the nicest thing anyone had ever done for her. 'I saw you getting into that car so that seemed all right, until I was nearly back at the hotel when I started wondering who had picked you up, what stranger's car you'd climbed into. And I knew I should have no peace until I'd satisfied myself you were home.'

Suddenly she was so buoyant with happiness that she could have been floating.

'So I parked near,' he said. 'And walked along the footpath and there was a light upstairs. You came to the window just as I was deciding to knock on the door and find out if you were safely back.'

She nearly said, 'I saw you,' but she hadn't. It had been too dark, she had just felt that he was out there; and if she had followed her instincts she could have run out and found him. She reached across the table and he took her hand in both his. She said, 'I'm so sorry, about everything.'

'It's been a rough passage. Do you know why I didn't phone you from France?' She shook her head. 'Because if I had done I should have said "Come over". I missed you that badly, that soon. And then Peter rang and told me about Jack Perry.'

She might have flinched but he held her hand steadily, clasping his strong fingers around hers. 'It

should have answered the questions but it didn't,'
he said. 'Even when you smiled and said "best forgotten" that we'd loved each other, you and I, I
felt murderous then but it still made no sense.'

Even when he should have hated her he was
caring about her, protecting her, and she looked at
him with misty eyes and thought, I believe I could
die for you.

'What happened in the lighthouse was real
whatever else had been pretence,' he said, 'And
when I got this letter this morning I thought that
if any of the rest could be explained I couldn't have
completely lost you.'

She wanted to jump over the table and throw
herself at him. She wanted him to grab her and kiss
her and stop talking so that she could stop talking
too. She said, 'Could we go somewhere more
comfortable? Please,' and in the hall she said,
'Upstairs?'

'Of course,' said Adam.

Flower stayed downstairs, stretched out on the
rug in front of the Aga. He knows I'm in safe
hands, thought Millie. She thought, how lovely that
the house is empty; and Amy said I was to have an
early night.

This was hardly the kind of early night Amy had
meant, and Millie bit down an almost hysterical
giggle. The swoosh from the depths of despair to
soaring joy had been so sudden and so fast that it
had left her reeling, and inside her bedroom she
was shaking when Adam's arms went round her.

Not with passion at first, just holding and
comforting her. She was weeping silently, her tears
must be soaking his jacket, because it had been

hellish and she couldn't believe it was over and that he loved her.

Or almost loved her. He held her as if she was precious to him, and he wiped her tears away and said, 'My sweet Millie.' She sniffed with a wobbly smile.

'I'm damping the chemistry down.'

'I love you, Millie,' he said.

He kissed her gently and she clung to him as the kisses became more urgent, and hungrier, until it seemed as if they were starving for the taste of each other.

'I missed you,' he said hoarsely. 'And I thought it would be for ever.'

It had seemed a long, long time, but now they were coming home and coming to life and they began to strip, taking off clothes, not taking their eyes from each other. He touched her shoulder as she bared it, briefly as though he was reassuring himself she was real, and she put out a hand against the hard flat stomach when he stood magnificently naked and they fell together on the bed.

This time there was nothing he had to teach her. The sensations and responses she had learned from him the first time were second nature to her now. She was on fire from the start. Everything was natural and rapturous, and the world shrank again to the circle of his arms and there were tears of joy in her eyes.

With him she was a demon lover, a tiger. It was so right, so mind-blowing. Like the last time in a bonding beyond the chemistry of sex she was with him and of him, blood of his blood, bone of his bone. Without him she would wither and die, and her fingers clutched the broad, muscular shoulders so tightly that her nails could be leaving scars.

No words, although she heard her name, whispered or groaned; and she wanted to get inside him and write her name on his heart as his was written on hers. She wanted to live and love for ever in this primitive paradise of passion and possession.

Hours later, it seemed, she lay, still warm and melting, in his arms, and he smiled down at her. 'Did the tower shake?'

'Always,' she said. Oh, lord, she loved him so. She would never get enough of his tenderness and toughness, his brilliant mind and his beautiful body. She let her head fall back, smiling, remembering.

'When we were talking in the lighthouse about if this was the world's last night I knew there was no one I'd rather spend it with than you.'

He lifted a damp tendril that was sticking to her forehead, kissed it and tucked it back behind her ear. 'I felt the same. That you were my world.'

After that there was a little silence. With her cheek resting on his chest she could feel him breathing, hear his heartbeats. She could have fallen asleep, curled up against him, and slept all through the night so long as he was lying beside her. She was safe at home so long as he was here.

She yawned and he said, 'I'm sacking you from the *Sentinel*.'

'Are you?'

'You could spend more time on your novel.'

'I could even start one.'

'Or I could offer you a roving commission.'

'As what?'

'My wife.' Their voices had been lazy and slow; his still was. 'You'd better marry me, Millie, because I can never let anyone else have you.'

She stirred then and sat up to look at him. 'Are we joking?'

He had to be and she waited for him to smile. Instead he seemed to change the subject. 'When you knew what I thought about your father's work, how did you know?'

That threw her. She floundered for words and he went on, 'Nobody reads my mind; I'm well known for my inscrutability.' Then he smiled so this wasn't serious. 'By the way, he was talented, but not as good as I was telling your mother. But how did you know?'

'I—just did,' she stammered.

He took her face in his hands. 'Then you know what I'm thinking now.' She looked into his eyes and the love she saw there enveloped her entirely.

She whispered, 'I think you had better marry me,' and he kissed her, sealing the moment like a vow.

A while later he asked, 'Where did that ring you wore going down to Cornwall come from?'

'My great-aunt Sophie left it to me in her will.'

'Well, tomorrow I get you a ring and you wear it on the right finger.'

'I would like that.' Down in the hall the phone started ringing and she sighed, 'Are bells ringing?'

'Unfortunately, yes. Let them.'

It could be Jack or it could be her mother. In either case if they got no answer they would try again and go on trying. 'Better get it over with,' she said, and slipped into a dressing-gown to answer it.

It was Jack and he got a very cool, 'Hello,' from Millie although he sounded less aggressive than last time.

He said, 'I wanted to tell you I've written to Schofield about your job, because he could well sack you. I could always find you something up here if you fancy it.'

'Not a lot,' said Millie.

'And if you want to tell him again I'm your brother I'll back you up on that.'

'Just get off the line,' she said, 'I'll ring you some time.' She would have to. Some time.

Adam had got into his trousers but barefooted and barechested he looked as he had in the lighthouse, standing now at the top of the stairs.

'Yes, it was Jack,' she said. 'He says he'll admit to being my brother.'

'Big of him. You can ring him tomorrow and tell him he's going to be mine.' And her eyes sparkled with malicious glee.

'That should terrify him.'

'We can but hope,' said Adam, and, laughing, Millie ran back upstairs into the arms of her love.

SUMMER SPECIAL!

**Four exciting new
Romances for the
price of three**

Each Romance features
British heroines and their
encounters with dark and
desirable Mediterranean
men. *Plus, a free
Elmlea recipe booklet
inside every pack.*

So sit back and enjoy
your sumptuous summer
reading pack and indulge
yourself with the free
Elmlea recipe ideas.

Available July 1994   Price £5.70

MILLS & BOON

*Available from WH Smith, John Menzies, Volume One, Forbuoys, Martins,
Woolworths, Tesco, Asda, Safeway and other paperback stockists.
Also available from Mills & Boon Reader Service, FREEPOST,
PO Box 236, Croydon, Surrey CR9 9EL. (UK Postage & Packing free)*

Full of Eastern Passion...

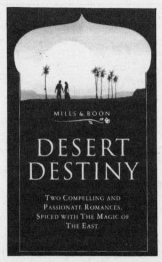

Savour the romance of the East this summer with
our two full-length compelling Romances,
wrapped together in one exciting volume.

AVAILABLE FROM 29 JULY 1994   PRICED £3.99

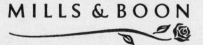

*Available from WH Smith, John Menzies, Volume One, Forbuoys, Martins,
Woolworths, Tesco, Asda, Safeway and other paperback stockists.
Also available from Mills & Boon Reader Service, FREEPOST,
PO Box 236, Croydon, Surrey CR9 9EL. (UK Postage & Packing free)*

Win a Year's Supply of romances
ABSOLUTELY FREE!

YES! you could win a whole year's supply of
Mills & Boon romances by playing the Treasure Trail Game.
Its simple! - there are seven separate items of treasure hidden
on the island, follow the instructions for each and when you arrive at the final
square, work out their grid positions, (i.e **D4**) and fill in the grid reference boxes.

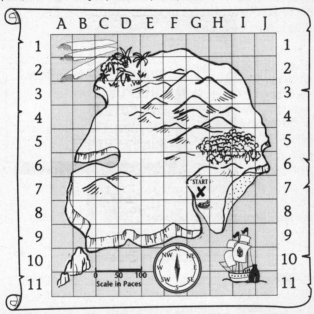

From the start, walk 250
paces to the **North**.

GRID REFERENCE

Now turn **West** and
walk 150 paces.

BRANDY

GRID REFERENCE

From this position walk
150 paces **South**.

GRID REFERENCE

Now take 100 paces **East**.

GRID REFERENCE

Then 100 **South**.

GRID REFERENCE

And finally 50
paces **East**.

GRID REFERENCE

Please turn over for entry details

SEND YOUR ENTRY
NOW!

The first five correct entries picked out of the bag after the closing date will each win one year's supply of Mills & Boon romances (six books every month for twelve months - worth over £90). What could be easier?

Don't forget to enter your name and address in the space below then put this page in an envelope and post it today (you don't need a stamp).

Competition closes 28th Feb '95.

TREASURE TRAIL Competition
FREEPOST
P.O. Box 236
Croydon
Surrey CR9 9EL

Are you a Reader Service subscriber?   Yes ☐   No ☐

Ms/Mrs/Miss/Mr _____ COMTT

Address _____

_____

_____

Postcode _____

Signature _____

One application per household. Offer valid only in U.K. and Eire. You may be mailed with offers from other reputable companies as a result of this application. Please tick box if you would prefer not to receive such offers. ☐